IOS

IOS

F/S

First published 1997

This anthology © 1997 by Bloomsbury Publishing Plc

The copyright of the individual contributions remains with the respective authors © 1997

The moral rights of the authors have been asserted

Bloomsbury Publishing Plc, 38 Soho Square, London W1V 5DF

A CIP catalogue record for this book is available from the British Library

ISBN 0 7475 3753 4

10 9 8 7 6 5 4 3 2 1

Typeset by Palimpsest Book Production Limited,
Polmont, Stirlingshire
Printed in Great Britain by Clays Ltd, St Ives plc

Contents

In September 1996 the *Independent on Sunday* asked readers to send in unpublished short stories of between 3,000 and 5,000 words for a competition, the prize for which was £500 and publication in the *Independent on Sunday*. We at Bloomsbury were celebrating our tenth anniversary with a collection of ten short stories by some of our most illustrious authors and felt to be associated with the prize was an appropriate way to mark the occasion and to encourage new writers in the form. Although we hoped we might discover some new talents we were not expecting a book to come out of it. We invited Margaret Atwood and Will Self to join Jan Dalley and me as judges and sat back for three months while typewriters and computers were clacking throughout the land.

From the eight hundred or so stories sent in we whittled the list down to five or six each. Only one story appeared on all four judges' shortlists and this was Joe O'Donnell's highly original and touching *Seraphim Preening*. So he got the cheque. Each of the judges had a different favourite and as many as fourteen were rated highly enough to encourage us to publish this collection. We were astonished at the high standard of the stories generally.

Publisher's Note

It says much for the readers of the *Independent*. It also shows that the short story form is in robust shape.

Margaret Atwood's list of what she was looking for might well have served as a guide for us all: 'Well written within its style. Convincing detail. Not too predictable. Story holds my attention. Story holds together. Originality. Believable within its genre. That intangible something.' Ah yes, that intangible something.

Will Self expressed a keen desire to be quickly involved by the story and favoured those which were tense, evocative, erotic, quirky and 'properly contemporary.' He especially liked *Memoirs of a White Slave* by Aleksandra Lech. Interestingly, the stories on each of our short lists were otherwise all different and each only gained one vote. Thus the tastes of the judges were as catholic as the stories themselves.

At a loss for a suitable title for this collection, we plumped for *IOS* in some desperation. Then we discovered the Greek goddess of that ilk (ignoring the slight spelling discrepancy): *EOS* – the Greek goddess of the dawn. At the end of each night she ascended to heaven in a chariot drawn by swift horses to announce the coming light of the sun. Though married to Tithonus, she carried off several beautiful youths. (Aphrodite had cursed her with an insatiable desire for young men.)

Make of that what you will. It might make a good short story at least.

LIZ CALDER
July 1997

Seraphim Preening | Joe O'Donnell

1 Be kind to your web-footed friends

I am a small man. I sit at the edge of my tiny cot bed, legs dangling over the end. I am subvocalising a march by the late John Philip Sousa. In fifty-four minutes I go to see the doctor.

Last Tuesday. I was making small figures from sheets of paper taken from a ream on my table. I think ream is the word. They were not simple figures. They were made with care and deliberation after a pattern I copied from an origami book in the prison library

When I launched them into the air they floated. How they floated! Some looped the loop. Others skidded between my legs under the cot bed. More crashed into the door of the cell.

After a while I could stand it no longer. I banged on the door. Again I banged. Very loudly. I called out. Louder still.

'Warder! Warder!'

I took a tin plate and clattered on the door.

'Warder! Warder!'

A single eye appeared in the peephole. A rattle of keys. The door slammed open.

'What is it dis time?'

Dese, dems and dose: he was an ugly culchie with bad breath.

'Me shoulders.'

'What's up with your shoulders?'

He was in a bad mood.

'The pain. Back again. I want to see a doctor.'

He vardied the cell. Saw the paper figures for the first time. Picked one up.

'What's all dis?'

'It's a bird.'

'What's it made of?'

'Paper.'

'And where did you get the paper, yeh little git?'

'From you, warder.'

'Yeh little git. You told me you wanted to write your bleedin' memoirs, and I bleedin' believed you, didn't I? Foolish-ate-yer-bun dat I am.'

He grabbed the tiny figures, crash-landed around the cell, and crushed them in his large raw-boned hairy-backed hands. He scooped up the rest of the – what was that word? – ream.

'Dat's it den. Made a bloody geheck of me.'

He stood at the door.

'You're a quare bloody hawk, d'ya know that? A quare bloody hawk.'

4

'What about the pains? In my shoulders?'

'Doctor comes on Friday. Stay in your cell. Keep your nose clean and I'll fix an appointment for you.'

He slammed the door. His footsteps down the corridor echoed to nothing.

I was going to write me memoirs. I really intended to. The paper birds were a ritual invocation to my anamnesis.

I'm Seraphim. Seraphim Coddles. Seraphim. I looked it up in a dictionary. It means celestial being, one of the highest order of the ninefold celestial hierarchy, gifted especially with love, and associated with light, love, ardour and purity. That's me. Light. Love. Ardour. And. Purity.

At school we learned about angels from the catechism. Seraphim, Cherubim, Thrones, Dominations, Principalities, Powers, Virtues, Archangels and Angels.

Angels ran in our family. Me father was Raphael, me granda's name was Gabriel. At night I'd sit up in bed and recite the names out loud.

'Seraphim, Cherubim, Thrones, Dominations, Principalities, Powers, Virtues, Archangels and Angels.'

They had wings and they swooped around heaven buzzing the clouds.

2   For a duck may be somebody's mother

Every Sunday morning my father would take me to the Bird Market.

'Straighten your shoulders,' he'd say, 'straighten your curse o' God shoulders and shame the world.'

Lofty red-brick buildings, tall and shabby, rabbit warrens for people. Under the shadow of St Patrick's Cathedral. A square of bitter grass where the old wither in the sun and the young play piggy in the shade of Swift.

My father had often talked of the Bird Market and I imagined it as a glass building, airy and spacious and ringing with the chatter and barter of bird and buyer.

It wasn't.

A shabby wicket in a lean-to falling-down gate.

'This is it,' my father said. 'The Bird Market.'

A narrow lane, evil-smelling and crammed with people. All I could make out were the pockets of coats and the big gnarled hands which occasionally dropped to top a fag or knock the dottle from a pipe. Couldn't see more.

When he was in a good mood me da would remedy this by hoisting me on his shoulders. I locked my hands beneath his chin and felt the sandpaper of his unshaven cheeks.

The birdcages were strung along one wall. Tiny cages full of the flurry of angel wings and raw wet beaks and black frenzied eyes. I saw them when he was in good humour. When he wasn't, I didn't.

'Da! Daaa!'

'Yis.'

'Can I have a bird? Of me own.'

'You're too young.'

'I'm six and three-quarters.'

'You're too young. You wouldn't look after it.'

On my tenth birthday I bought a bird. A cock linnet. The dealer put it in a little brown paper bag with holes in it.

Me da wasn't pleased.

'What's in the bag?'

'It's nothing, Da.'

'Give it here.' His large raw-boned hairy-backed hands tore open the paper. His fingers closed around the bird. I could see the tiny chest thumping between those fingers.

'Where'd you get this?'

I told him.

'How much?'

I told him.

He went spare.

'Five bob! That was the money yer granda Gabriel gave yeh for your birthday.'

'I know –'

'The money I told you to put into the post office.'

'I know, Da, but I'll save up –'

'It was to be put in the post office and you bought a bloody bird with it.'

'I wanted one. Of me own.'

I knew I was snivelling. My father hated snivelling. He waved the bird under my nose. His tone was pleading and reasonable.

'When I tell you to do something you must obey. The fourth commandment. Honour thy father and thy mother. If you disobey you must be punished.'

He didn't punish me. He punished the fucking bird. He wrung its neck. I gave it a sailor's burial. I set it in a matchbox out to sea.

I was obedient after that.

When he said I was to go to work in the timber yard, I went to work in the timber yard.

He carried me on the crossbar of his bike. My legs, being tiny, got pins and needles. It nearly friggin' crippled me.

'It's a good job,' he said, 'a good job with prospects.'

Good job? Messenger boy more like. Fifteen bob a week. I got on well with the others, kept me nose clean, and after five years rose to the exalted rank of junior docket clerk. I was twenty-one. My father died. I rode his bike.

My legs – never my most becoming feature – didn't quite reach the pedals and to ride it I had to roll from side to side. The kids made an awful jeer of me.

'Eh . . . stand on tuppence to look over thruppence.'

Or 'Little oul' fellah cut short.'

My legs were too short for the pedals and my mind was too slow for the speed of the orders in the timber yard where I worked.

'Docket this, Coddles, load waiting checker's standing out in the rain get the finger out me lorry's tickin' over I need the docket now here's the mill return twenty twelves nine by four two deeps one flat your father would've done it in his head hurry it up hurry it up Jasus this half-eegit's not half the man his father was . . .'

3   Be kind to the denizens of the swamp

The other clerks tended to pick on me.

'Have a nice weekend then? With the birds again?'

I explained that that was how I spent my Sunday. Up to the Market after Mass and stayed there till the pub opened. Then the dealers left and I went home to my books.

They made a lot of play about me having a 'bird'. I'm no fool. I knew what they were at. It pleased me to indulge them.

'Ever had a bird, Coddles? Of your own?'

'Yis.'

'What was it like?'

'Trembled in my hand.'

A nudge. A smirk.

'Then died.'

A snort of laughter.

'I set it in a matchbox out to sea.'

All the time they'd make the same jokes, ask the same questions.

'How's the pains in your shoulders?'

'Still there.'

'It's that bloody bike. Why don't you buy yourself a little model?'

'That bike was belong to my father.'

And that was the end of that.

I went for a job as commercial rep. for the company. I was the best qualified but they turned me down because of my height. O'Toole, the manager, even allowed himself a little joke as he cracked the knuckles of his large raw-boned hairy-backed hands.

'You're ideal, Coddles,' he said, 'except in one small detail. As you are aware, appearance is of the utmost importance.'

I knew what was coming.

'So you will appreciate,' he chuckled, 'that in this vital quali- fication you fall short, if I may allow myself a little joke.'

Gobshite. The pains in my shoulders got worse.

I never married. It was shortly after being turned down for the job that the Helen episode occurred, I believe. And it was Nolan, the one who eventually got the traveller's job, who set me up.

A new assistant orders clerk, by name Helen Moraghan, had been engaged at head office and I grew to know her – purely because we phoned one another all the time on business.

Nolan told me that Helen was about my size. I'd never met her. She was just a pleasant daily voice on the order phone.

'Knee-high to a gin bottle,' said Nolan, 'and she seems struck on you.'

The next time she rang down from the office, with a request, I remember, for seven by one tongued and grooved, I took my courage in both my hands.

'Oh by the way, Helen. That is, would you be interested in coming, that is if you've nothing better to do? I mean I thought you and me like might, if you're free . . . If you'd like to that is.'

Yes, she said, she'd like that. Yes, she said, she'd see me Friday night. The Metropole. Half seven.

It was as easy as that.

Dearest, dearest Helen. Half past seven, outside the Metropole.

A wet Friday evening. Newsboys still crying out the evening papers.

'*Herald a' Mail, Herald a' Mail!*'

The Metropole clock struck the half hour.

I looked in front of me. Long legs. Long long legs leading all the way up past a long slender figure. Somewhere up there a heart-shaped face framed in black curls glittering with the diamonds of rain and topped with a jellybag hat smiled down on me.

'Helen?'

'Seraphim?'

I nodded, dumb with misery and cold with rain.

She was tall. Very tall. I suppose it was funny, if you had Nolan's sense of humour. She was kind. Very kind. She was also very embarrassed, particularly when at the pictures I had to sit on a tipped-up seat to see over the head of the person in front.

And no, she said, no she didn't feel like having a Knickerbocker Glory in the Palm Grove.

I didn't ask her out again. Nor did we continue our chatty little conversations. She was transferred to O'Toole's personal office. I neither saw nor heard of her after that. And the pains were very severe.

'Docket this, Coddles, load waiting checker's standing out in the rain get the finger out me lorry's tickin' over I need the docket now wrong timber T and G we sent him P and J they'll fall through the fucken floor if they use that hurry it up Jasus this half-eegit's not half the man his father was . . .'

4   Where the weather is cold and damp

Eventually I was kicked out. In 1945 during the builders' strike. The clerical staff were not members of the union. I was afraid of losing my job. But I was afraid of the pickets as well. The first day I reported for duty I passed them. We all did. No business that day, all day. Me I just sat on my backside and read *Birds of the World** till it was time to go home.

Then . . .

Then I found they had slashed the tyres of my father's bike.

'Yiz shower of cunts.'

'Listen, son, that's just a warning.'

I went for the nearest one.

'Yiz fucken scum of the fucken earth. My da – '

He held me at arm's length.

---

* By Oliver Austin, published by Golden Press, New York and, alas, now long out of print.

'Your father got his head broke open by a bobby's baton in nineteen twelve. Raphael Coddles was no scab.'

I went home. Took to me bed. I didn't get up for a week. The strike continued for six. The letter from O'Toole put the tin hat on my career in the world of the builders' providers.

'Blah, blah, blah,' he wrote, 'blah, blah, blah, your contract is considered to be terminated.'

I got up to read the letter. I went back to bed when I had finished it.

I went to bed a young man. I rose from it an old man. An old man in an older city. My love contracted to a small – radius, I think is the word. I didn't have much time for people. Only for birds. And I was never short of their company.

In this city there are plenty of birds. The gush and gabble of a thousand starlings in O'Connell Street, eternally scolding, eternally noisy. Birds in the Phoenix Park: great-crested grebes, mallards, moorhens, collared doves, pied wagtails, song thrushes, starlings, sedge warblers, tits (long-tailed, coal, blue and great), jackdaws, magpies, linnets, yellowhammers, and the little wren known in Gaelic as *dreolin* or in Latin as *Troglodytes troglodytes*.

Oftimes I did think of myself as *Troglodytes troglodytes*.

A poet or some such irresponsible person once wrote:

A Robin Redbreast in a cage
Puts all Heaven in a Rage.

Any bird in any cage certainly put me in a rage. Anywhere

there were birds you could expect to find me. Anywhere there were birds in cages you could expect trouble.

Sooner or later.

Birds in cages.

(For the record: my father wrung the neck of a cock linnet. I gave him a sailor's burial. I set him in a matchbox out to sea.)

Timber I scavenged off the building sites, and God knows there were enough of them. Whole sections of our fair city were being torn down in jig time and there was always timber: tongued and grooved, planed and joined, planed all over, oh my early training came in handy and no mistake. Also nails to be knocked off. A Stanley knife. Even a small handsaw. Carefully I made it. Some two foot six by two foot six by four foot with two large leather straps which fitted over my shoulders. In it were bored a series of holes approximately one inch in diameter.

I had it figured out. The Bird Market held caged birds. To open the cages was out of the question.

Wall high. Seraphim low.

Besides there were too many people about who might legitimately be expected to object. There was no way to get them except by buying them. Money: that was what was needed. In the final analysis.

Money.

The dole wouldn't buy much. Not at current prices. And if I bought a single bird, me da'd probably rise from the grave and wring its neck.

Near the market was a pet shop. The sign said: *Aenghus*

MacGiollaphib. For a long time I thought his name was Anus. That's how he pronounced it. It tickled me to think of so aptly named an arsehole. It wasn't until I saw it gilt-lettered above his shop. *Aenghus MacGiollaphib*. Pets. Somebody had spray-painted on underneath: farm fresh, nutritious and delicious.

The owner didn't like me.

'It's you again.'

'I'm a cash customer.'

He peered through the shutters of the door.

'Piss off, I'm closed.'

I showed him the money.

'Look, I've got money. Five shillings.'

'What do you want, yeh little git?'

'I'd like some millet, and a cuttlefish bone.'

He drew the bolt and opened the door a crack.

'Now stay right there. And no monkey business, d'yeh hear? I've got to go into the store for it.'

He went into the store. His big mistake was leaving his keys on the counter. I locked him in the storeroom. Then I opened the cash register.

He started to bang on the door.

'Hey, what are you up to? Silly bugger. I'll have the law on you. Let me out, now, you oul' eegit.'

I scooped the jackpot that morning. Twenty-five quid and change. I still had twenty minutes. Five minutes to get to the Market and fifteen minutes to make my purchases.

'The cock linnets is five bob a skull.'

'How many yeh got?'

'Eight.'

'I'll take the lot.'

Linnets, bullfinches, chaffinches, even a fucken macaw I bought.

'How much is the canary?'

'Thirty bob and that includes the cage.'

'Gimme the bird, and you can stick your cage.'

In they went. Into the box. They thought I was mad. In the Market. I left them gob-smacked with their backs to the empty cages.

The box was heavy and throbbing with fluttery life as I trudged down the Quays towards the Fifteen Acres. The edges of the timber lay heavy and sore on shoulder and back. I knew how the late Jesus Christ must have felt going up that hill.

Beside the Wellington Monument I stopped. I placed the box carefully on the ground. It was a grand day. A pet day. I took me time. The kids gathered around. To jeer. I couldn't give a shit for their jibes.

'Eh, mister, what's in the box?'

'Will yeh open the box or take the money?'

'Were you always that small or did your mother leave you out in the rain all night?'

Suddenly I whipped out the Stanley knife. Be Jasus that scattered them. They stood in a wide and cautious circle around me.

Out on the road I could see a police car with its blue light flashing. Two large Civic Guards got out of the car and began to run towards me. I waited until they were yards away then

I slit the leather fastening with me knife and tipped open the lid.

The birds volcanoed upwards, shit and feathers flying far and wide. It was a magnificent sight. The kids fell back. Even the Guards stood awed.

When the birds had found their freedom the Guards escorted me to the car. I have never known such peace in my life.

5 Now, you may think that this is the end

My name is Seraphim Coddles and I am in prison. I sit on my bunk bed with my legs dangling over the side. I have just come back from the doctor. The warder enters. Without knocking.

'What did he say? The doctor.'

'He said there's nothing organically wrong. Gave me a bottle to rub in. He'll see me again in a week's time if the pains don't go.'

The warder looks at me.

'Are you worried?'

'Wouldn't you be?'

The warder suddenly starts to chuckle to himself.

'God and Mighty,' says the culshie bastard, 'the only ting I can tink of is dat you're sprouting a pair of wings. Hah.'

He pounds the edge of the bunk with his fist. His large raw-boned hairy-backed fist. I bounce up and down.

'Dat's a good one, eh? A bloody good one. A bloody pair of wings. I must tell the lads . . .'

Joe O'Donnell

He is still laughing as he leaves.
I worry for him.
I think he should be locked up.
Possibly in a cage.
If this strikes you, as it struck me, as madness . . .

6   Well, it is . . .

Memoirs of a White Slave | Aleksandra Lech

I can't explain it, can't describe him at all really. If the authorities ever caught up with me I'd be hard pushed to provide a profile. He was dark; he had dark hair and eyes. The eyes were opaque, impenetrable . . . I remember his penis, of which he was rightly proud, because I'd never seen a circumcised penis before. I remember it for this and other qualities. I remember some but not all of the things we did together. We rarely spoke, there wasn't time. We meant to, but the sex was clamorous, it just had to be addressed. Valuing words, I tried writing to him, but my letters were intercepted. At the time I thought of another woman, but now I suspect his vast extended family, who were everywhere.

The daily routine was mundane enough. In the morning I did the chores, then I was free to take breakfast and loaf around, although I soon learnt to avoid afternoon naps. The time of year, though, didn't help, and on dull days I was left with an impression of him, like the smell of someone that lingers long after they've left the room. I envied the children who laughed and jostled outside, acting out their savagery on each other.

He'd consumed so much of me with his big appetite and his urgent needs, I'd become inert, a food that no longer has any taste, pushed to the side of the plate.

Sometimes, though, very late at night, he'd creep into the kitchen and down a full bottle of Spanish red. He had to do this clandestinely, on account of the fact that he was teetotal. Then later he urinated on my dreams. Lying foetally, the side of my head hot and moist, I felt the warm liquid spread on to the pillow.

'I love your breasts,' he'd murmured, prompting a startled 'Pardon?' from me. How could he even locate them? Latent paedophilia clearly had me in its thrall. I hardly dared confess my age – I had a full four years on him, despite his apparent seniority. He was unquestionably the more experienced of the two of us, and he had that attractive ravaged thing certain men acquire in maturity. He also had the knack of winding me up. Then it was amazing where I'd spring to. Several times I found myself bouncing up and down near the ceiling, and once I mounted the bathroom sink and from there slid down into the stagnating bathwater (he never unplugged anything), where I gaped and gurgled like a fish. Tiring of these antics, I made plans to escape up into the loft and hide out there for a while, but he got wind of this, tore up the blueprint, and folded up the loft ladder with his teeth. Up till then I'd only seen such feats performed by circus acrobats. He had my admiration, and my fear, just as a despot might, but I was cruel in little ways, and expert at hiding my true feelings, which nearly drove him crazy. He wanted them, wanted them, but not me, not in that way, only to eat and dive into and maybe savour for a while. In order to appease him, and for the pleasure it gave me, I became expert at cooking little dishes, things I knew he'd like, but although appreciative he behaved as though they'd arrived magically from nowhere, reminding me of that royal household where eggs are cooked ceaselessly, three minutes a go, in order to be forever fresh and ready for the Prince's arrival.

Eventually he became so angry and jealous that one day he announced that only he was allowed to do the cooking, having already arranged it so that he would personally oversee the carnage in the slaughterhouse, marking out each lamb with some hieroglyphic of his own invention as it went through the turnstile. When finally we sat down I ate up the meal – his careful inspections had paid off and the meat was unbelievably tender. Long after he'd finished I carried on sitting there at the table, the bit, as it were, between my teeth, savouring each morsel. He saw exactly what was happening, and decided to put me on a diet of sugared baby food, which I was force-fed through a tube. My appetite dwindled; I wept when I remembered the sweet and subtle dishes we'd shared together in the past. I grew thin, so he employed a woman whose job he told me was to fatten me up, get me right and out again. Meanwhile, he went off somewhere without telling me. He came back later to collect the woman, they needed time alone together he said, and left me with a number which I was to call if I wanted anything. I tried committing it to memory, but the zeros hung around meaninglessly and the sixes became nines, threes coupled into figures of eight; the whole thing was a mess and eventually I just gave up the ghost, never thinking that the ghost had no intention of relinquishing me. Ugly thing, he had me in his fat embrace; his clammy grasp ruined my chances of ever getting well again and taking up a normal healthy girl's life of boyfriends and tennis – my mother's dream.

Actually his body was a temple, but definitely Islamic, squat and rounded with absolutely no graven images in sight. When I held him tight I could feel the blood boiling inside his skin. I began to see that in him beauty and ugliness were one, as happens sometimes in the natural world, and like nature he was both sacred and profane in his tastes and habits. He liked to talk about herdsmen and talismans and popular revolt, he discouraged interjection, hated interruption of any kind, and once he'd made the initial exploratory study of me, which was quick and intensive, he quit looking into my mind altogether, and hardly thought of me except as a vehicle for those improvised rides.

I saw how the land lay; I was his pony. Whenever I spoke out loud he looked positively shaken, as though the sound had emanated from some inanimate object, a chair or earthenware pot or something, or from a deep well or the tall tree outside our window. Startled out of his reverie, I think he would have been less surprised if the palace dogs had struck up a conversation. I thought I understood his moods, and wished above all else that he could read my mind and cut through all this crap of self-expression, explanation, and informed opinion. Perhaps to soothe his shattered nerves, he insisted on music everywhere, so we woke and washed and made love to a constant running soundtrack, endless tapes of singing and slide guitar which frankly I could have done without. I'm a music lover myself, but not twenty-four hours a day non-stop, even the birds quit their twittering every now and then. Unlike the guard dogs, whose incessant barking reverberated round the quad both day and night. I tried turning the music up, to drown out the cacophony, but the higher the volume, the more a malevolent sibilance could be heard underscoring everything – the rasped hissing of angry geese.

The women kept to the upper chamber, as tradition demanded, padding about barefoot and veiled like Turkish odalisques. Actually it was surprisingly cosy up there, a kind of sewing circle without the doilies and the cups of tea, language was certainly no barrier; we all knew exactly what we had in common. But when I rebelled the punishment was swift and ruthless. My bright pink chiffon scarf was confiscated, and I was led to the bathroom, stripped of all my privileges, and made to sit in the corridor by myself for hours on end. My chair – they'd given me a chair, they weren't unkind – was by the toilets, so at least I was able to watch people come and go, and in the end I got quite used to the sounds of farting, the splashing urinals and the groaning, climactic shits. People were generally a bit shifty with me, knowing what I knew; they felt faintly compromised by my presence, although word spread of my murky past, and they soon learnt to ignore me, so much so that to save themselves time they often emerged unbuttoned, hoisting themselves up and girding their loins as they passed. In this way I discovered a vocation for the invisible life.

His *mullah* status afforded him a very Eastern notion of time. In other words, he was late for everything – by hours and hours. Sometimes a whole day went round again before he made his appointment. He liked to travel with a whole entourage of people, he loved women of course but basically anyone was welcome to join this lengthening, unwieldy caravan. In the evening all he wanted to hear was *Arabian Nights*, he hated my 'Under Western Skies' approach and the cool, modern language I employed. When I mentioned computers it nearly drove him crazy. He decided that I was impossible, beyond the pale, and would have no more of me, unless I was undressed or wearing Marks and Spencer's underwear. Sometimes though, if I kept very quiet, I was allowed to put on my big Burberry and we'd go as a treat to Harrods Emporium, where he'd forget his loathing for modern currencies (never mind plastic) and indulge his delight in novelty watches. His favourite featured a crowing cockerel, which I found slightly sinister and potentially insane in a bathetic, *Blue Angel*-type way. Once, after he'd inflicted a particularly deep wound via a third party, I asked him whether it crowed three times on special occasions, but being non-Christian the analogy was lost on him, and he just gave me one of his long inscrutable stares. He had a deep respect, though, for all religions and belief systems, what he hated was my pragmatism and a form of hilarious resignation I'd adopted, actually a smokescreen for my rather fanciful take on life. He wanted romance with a capital R and the licence to practise it anywhere at any time with the partner of his choice. He hated the idea that sex might be linked to survival, that there was anything at all calculating about relationships sent him into a holy rage of moral indignation which blew on for days.

Although he despised American decadence, he loved the all-American fallen heroes, and one time we went to see *The Wild Bunch*, where we both instantly fell in love with William Holden. I liked the film for what it chose to reveal about the male psyche, I didn't find it exploitative in any way, I thought the prostitutes were grand. After ten minutes of hearing me expound, which he suffered in an explosive silence, he banished the subject of cowboys and whores from the conversation, on pain of death-by-expulsion. This didn't surprise me; whenever his women talked of sexual abuse and harassment he left the room, or tried to silence them. I think perhaps it turned him on, and obviously he felt uncomfortable with this.

The bedroom was so vast that we set up a massive tent in there and furnished it luxuriously, rug on rug. The makeshift *yurt* gave off a whiff of the nomadic life, although I could never quite decide which desert we were in, Mojave or Badiet esh Sham. On the Sunday I went to the market and bought the finest-quality kilims to drape over our bed. Everywhere was hung with fabric, and the warm glowing reds, the luminous saffrons, deep indigos and cobalt blues complemented his gorgeous skin tones and oily black hair. Once when I looked at him his eyes shone out a radiance I'd never seen there before. At least, I think it was him; there were so many faces, and the place was so crowded and so underlit, it was hard to discern his features amongst so many others. I'd just come back from the M&S food hall, carting bags and bags of shopping, and the dim candlelight was dazzling after the dayglo fluorescence of the store. As my eyes readjusted I started to make out men's faces in the gloom, and began to feel myself as I must seem to them, small and white and uncertain. Later that night I said to him, Imagine if we could swap bodies, just for an instant, what it must feel like to be inside your skin, how you might feel in me. He laughed indulgently at this, exposing the gold cap on his tooth, and pointed out that the operation had been accomplished as far as he was concerned, but that wasn't quite what I meant, although sometimes perhaps it came close. It's impossible to know for sure, whether what seems profoundly to be true really is so for the other person, never mind objective truth, which either doesn't exist or else obliterates us, that one-eyed undertaker with the hole in his head where the moon shines through. As for camaraderie, I sometimes felt the despair of my sex, that equality can never come, because the differences are too profound; at least black and white are the same under their surface branding, history notwithstanding, the men share the same pumping organs, the same basic predilections. But, crossing the great divide . . . These endless negotiations, wearisome circumlocutions, were they ultimately only to build bridges over a desert? – I began to understand the Bedouin's respect for water, and I too felt that longing to be quenched, to watch the broad river flowing between my feet.

There was another room, a kind of recess with an earth-coloured curtain instead of a door, where I chose to hang out from time to time. Since no one else bothered with the place I came to think of it as mine, even crashing there some nights, but whenever I slept alone he became distrustful; he couldn't understand my bouts of solitude and thought that I should either be with him, or else with the women. One night he even sent a helicopter, which hovered outside my window like a huge noisy fly. I could see what it was that he was trying to tell me, and I really did want to be close. But his novelty watches got me down, and sometimes I simply had to take off. Because he'd never worked out how to set the cockerel, he'd bought umpteen duplicates and had them timed to go off at various intervals, which put your average radio alarm in the shade, I can tell you. Six o'clock, seven, eight in the morning, worse than a chicken coop, there it would be, the triumphant, cocky crowing, accompanied by an all-American modulated female voice, a kind of replicant speaking clock. Somehow he remained oblivious to these wake-up calls, it was only I who lived the nightmare of the simulated barnyard life, while he snored softly, his breath alone enough to turn me on in the intervals between the hourly blastings.

He took to travelling in a stretch limo, he loved to cruise around in it at night, and we'd invariably end up on the Bayswater Road, sitting in the back seat and eating sweet honeyed sesame cake until two or three in the morning. The smoked glass afforded us absolute privacy, we opted not to roll it down even though we were tempted by the incredibly slick movement it made. Towards the end we spent so much time in there – mostly, I admit, just playing with the gadgets – it became a kind of mobile home for us. Sometimes we'd all ride in the back, but we also took it more or less in turns to do the driving, although we weren't into strict rotas or anything like that, we just played it by ear and went with the flow. It felt strange, sitting naked behind the steering wheel, but he got such a kick out of seeing out where no one could see in, I didn't like to spoil his fun by being an old stick-in-the-mud. Besides, I was as excited as he was, I too loved the bright colourful shop windows, the city lights reflected in the freshly washed streets, the (best of all) people-watching. Our routes afforded us the most entertaining viewing, the most brilliant sightseeing tours ever. Crowds stared back at us astonished as our never-ending vehicle prowled on and on anamorphically, taking for ever to clear the street; pedestrians gaped across in such amazement I wondered sometimes how they would have responded if they'd had a privileged view *in*. Some laughed, some frowned to see us, but not *us*, although sometimes I felt a certain shiver as a man or woman with X-ray eyes appeared to do just that. For me it was reversed; I saw the outside of the car so rarely, I began to think of it as black, like the interior upholstery, and got quite a shock when I stepped out one morning to buy some cigarettes and, re-crossing the road, glanced over to see the thick milky-white bodywork gleaming in the fragile grey dawn. It touched me, for some reason, the sight of the limo sitting there, parked up against the kerb. It seemed to reflect my state of mind, invulnerable and exposed, like when you shed your clothes after the longest period of being bundled up in them, after a few days at a festival say, and finally at long last your skin can breathe. Curious, nevertheless, how moving objects can be, what sway they can hold over our emotions. Sometimes I'd just say the word to myself: stretch. Or the whole thing, stretch limo. Or, stretch marks. I began to enjoy the way my body was changing, I took a new interest in its little idiosyncrasies, and started to really notice just how different it looked, depending on time of day or month. His was less mutable, more constant, which was incredibly reassuring, but I especially loved it when he'd had a particularly hearty meal and his belly grew full and round. Then he was so substantial, so real and *out there*. The cataclysmic change that took place in him and wiped the floor with both of us simply served, paradoxically, to confirm that, and we climaxed on his affirmation.

After we completed our grand tour of Africa I got back in touch with my relatives, who replied at once with reams of meticulously handwritten pages, fluttering out of flimsy airmail envelopes like autumn leaves. Their contents told of walls turned to rubble, of iron curtains ripped painfully to shreds. Pausing from my reading, I gazed idly out of the window, and there gazing back at me was an urchin boy with an old man's face and thin, bandy legs, standing next to a scullery maid who wore a shy apologetic smile and voluminous grey skirts. When they saw that I'd seen them they waved their little monochrome Union Jacks, and raised a small cheer. The window rattled, a gust of wind blew in, and all the letters started to fly around my desk, so I gathered them up and set them under a paperweight, a big knotted root which had found its way from Ethiopia via Cairo and on to our boat.

I blame myself for his going away; it was me, after all, who'd exposed him to Western values, and eventually he became a stern disciple of, of all things, the white Anglo-Saxon work ethic. 'I'm a workaholic,' he announced balefully one day over breakfast, and left immediately to practise his new-found religion in the old country, where I gather it rather took off. I wanted something of him, a piece of clothing with his smell, like a comfort blanket, but all he left me was a videotape of himself inside a shopping mall, smiling to camera and explaining the philosophy behind the store's policy on customer choice, shoplifting, corporate service logos and the like. It was his image, but without the breathing (the store's muzak obliterated that – it was Christmas and there was much rejoicing around Santa's sleigh), without the touch of skin and the hot rush of blood, it meant nothing to me.

The men and women of the palace still go about their daily business. The mosque still wails out its ululations exhorting sinners to prayer. But that savage holy sheikh, sultan of days and nights, has ultimately been tamed, not by the law, not by a woman, not by anything save work and commerce and the WASP's dream of dreamless sleep, where morning crows triumphant. So; I'm the keeper of his demons, the dreamer of his dreams, I watch as the dark flame burns in the dead of night, and I'm no longer woken by a mad cockerel with a will all its own and a battery of bantam back-ups. My sleep, when disturbed, is broken by thoughts of an enduring kiss, of skin as soft as Persian silk, and of the tender blade of love that turned inside me but never drew blood. In these dark days of winter I sometimes fall into a troubled sleep, and, consumed by dreams, I have the lucid sense of being eaten alive. But then I relax; I taste fine, and, caged once more in my lover's arms, am animal again.

Welcome Back | Patrick Cunningham

We were a happy and united family until the day my sister Imelda gave birth to the reincarnation of Clement Attlee. That was when our troubles began.

It fell to me to make the announcement because I was the one who recognised him. On the evening after the birth I went into the ward at St George's, Tooting, a bunch of freesias in my hand, and I looked at my new nephew, my only nephew, lying in what seemed like a plastic milk crate. 'Clement Attlee,' I said.

Imelda was sitting up in bed, her hair newly washed, looking pleased with herself. By her side was her husband Raymond, looking even more pleased, and by Raymond's side was his brother Psycho Dave, who had come along to support him. My mother was sitting opposite; she looked pleased too.

'Clement Attlee,' I said.

'Looks more like Mao Tse-tung,' Psycho Dave said.

'Not looks like – *is*,' I said.

I had never considered reincarnation before, but now it was as though someone had put an information disk into my head that contained all I needed to know. There was not a shred of doubt in my mind. 'He's Clement Attlee,' I repeated.

No one took much notice of what I'd said. They thought I was suggesting a name for the child. They thought I was joshing.

I didn't pursue the matter just then; it didn't seem the right moment. I thought it best to bide my time.

Later that evening, back at the house, I got Raymond alone. I thought he, as the father, ought to be the first to know.

'Ray, that baby's the reincarnation of Clement Attlee,' I said.

Ray pondered my words for several moments. 'Is it something religious, sort of?' he asked.

'Pertaining to,' I said.

'Does that mean yes?'

'Sort of,' I said.

Raymond said no more. His face took on that trance-like expression that told me he was thinking deeply.

The first time Imelda was about to bring Ray to the house she said of him: 'He's a bit thick, but he's lovely.' Raymond was in fact very thick and he was, indeed, lovely. He had a sweet nature and he made Imelda happy and secure. Other young blokes with better brains had made her very unhappy and very insecure. 'Men are best when they're not too complicated,' she said.

My mother was doing a big washing-up when I told her. All the relations had come back to the house after visiting Imelda and the new baby and there was a mountain of crockery on the draining board. I was drying up and I slid the information casually into the conversation so as not to alarm her.

My mother, who does not like nonsense and does not like politicians, did not stop what she was doing. She squirted more detergent than was necessary into the sink and told me to stop talking nonsense. She said that the baby wasn't a reincarnation at all, but that if he was a reincarnation, then he wasn't a reincarnation of Clement Attlee and that if he was a reincarnation of Clement Attlee then it was because Clement Attlee had seen the error of his ways and had come back to undo the harm he had done. 'You should stop talking nonsense,' she repeated. 'You're an educated boy.'

I hated it when she called me an educated boy. I didn't feel educated. I was glad that I'd given her and my father the pleasure of my graduation day – especially since he'd died the following year – but I didn't feel that my three years at college had given me the added value my mother supposed. It hadn't trained me to be the leader of my family, which was what she'd hoped for. It hadn't made me a repository of all the world's knowledge.

I offered to sweep the kitchen floor, which is no small job. The kitchen is huge, as are all the rooms in the house. Double fronted, with four floors and a basement, it was my father's dream. It was also an example of his habit of biting off more than he could chew. He bought it cheaply because of the dilapidations and because of Mr Cranch, the sitting tenant, who occupied the big bay-windowed room on the first floor. My father was gone now, but Mr Cranch was still there and the house was still the warren of bed-sits and tiny flatlets it had been when he'd bought it. His grand plan of securing his family's future by converting it into beautiful flats had been passed on to me as my heritage.

We said no more until all the crockery was washed and dried and put away and the kitchen was tidy again. Then my mother said: 'If the baby is – what you say, then it's best to say nothing about it. You know what Raymond's family are like and you know what your father's side of the family are like, so the least they know the better. There's never been a hint of a reincarnation on my side of the family. First time round, all of us were.'

'They'll find out sooner or later,' I said.

'Later's best,' she said.

Imelda was alone with the baby when I called at the hospital the following evening. It struck me then that I'd felt no surprise on discovering that my nephew was the reincarnation of Clement Attlee and I felt no surprise now. He was asleep in his plastic crate and it seemed a nourishing kind of sleep as if it were building him up for what lay in the future.

'What kind of ideas have you been putting into Ray's head?' Imelda asked, giving me her elder-sister look.

'It's nothing to worry about,' I said. 'You've got a lovely healthy baby and he's the reincarnation of Clement Attlee and apart from that he's just like any other little tot. End of story.'

'Well, if he is,' she said, 'and I'm not saying I believe you, what are we supposed to do about it?'

'I don't know,' I said. 'You don't have to do anything about it if you don't want to.'

'But shouldn't we report it? Shouldn't we let someone know?'

'You could mention it to the health visitor, I suppose. It'd be her province.'

'I'll do that,' she said, 'just to set my mind at rest. You don't think it's my fault, do you – or Ray's?'

'Of course not,' I said. 'It could happen to anyone.'

'Not that I really believe it,' she said.

Imelda and the baby came home the next afternoon. She and Raymond had the flat on the first floor, opposite Mr Cranch's room. Psycho Dave had a bed-sit on the floor above. He had been made homeless when his parents emigrated to Australia, probably to get away from him, though they said it was to be near their daughter who was married in Melbourne. Psycho Dave had a habit of kicking down doors when he got upset. 'He don't mean nothing bad by it,' Raymond assured us. Raymond was devoted to his brother. We didn't find Dave's habit as inconvenient as his parents had because, being in the building trade, we always keep a few panelled doors in the back shed. You can find them easily enough in builders' skips and whenever I come across one I always take it home.

Psycho Dave and Ray paid no rent for their accommodation. Ray was a plumber and Dave an electrician and the strategy was that they would help me with the refurbishment of the house whenever they had time to spare. It worked well enough, but none of us had much time to give to the house and it remained a warren of bare rooms, exposed plaster, bare boards, with here and there little areas of comfort where one of us had tried to make a nest. Imelda and Raymond had the cosiest nest and we were busy preparing a room for the baby. They had called him John, after my father, but I could only see him as little Clem.

The baby didn't settle when Imelda brought him home. He couldn't seem to find contentment. His uncoordinated little arms and legs flailed about and his face became red with anguish. His reproachful wails went from a high note to a low. Everyone felt his misery.

I suggested to my mother that perhaps it was Clement Attlee expressing his dismay at finding the country in such a state.

'In that case,' my mother said, 'he'd do better to stop bawling and let us all get a good night's sleep.' She said that I was talking nonsense, that each baby had his own temperament and that some were easier than others. 'You wouldn't feed,' she accused me. 'Your weight kept going down instead of up. You had us frantic with worry.'

I said I was sorry for the inconvenience caused and she said that so I should be. I didn't bother her with any more opinions on the subject of little Clem.

Mr Cranch, the sitting tenant, complained that his nights were disturbed by the crying of little Clem. Mr Cranch made no noise whatever in his room. When he had first come to live there, twenty years before, the housekeeper in charge of the bed-sitting-rooms insisted on absolute quiet, and it had remained a lifetime habit. He owned neither radio nor television and seemed to go into a state of suspended animation when he closed the door of his room behind him. So he was particularly aggrieved that this new arrival should cause him sleepless nights. When I told him that the baby was the reincarnation of Clement

Attlee he said he wanted nothing to do with spooky things. He said he'd once stayed in a house where the landlady went in for Ouija boards and table-rapping with results that would make my hair stand on end if he cared to tell me about them. After that he avoided Imelda and the baby and scuttled into his room whenever he encountered them on the landing.

After several weeks of deep thought, Raymond consulted me again. 'Who was this Clement Attlee bloke, anyway?' he asked. 'I know the name but I can't put a face.'

'He was a politician,' I said.

'So he wasn't a boxer, then?'

'Not that I know of.'

'Only his name sounds like one of them American boxers,' Raymond said.

'Clement means mild or merciful,' I said. 'Hardly a suitable name for a boxer.'

'They could've given him that name just to put people off their guard.'

'You have a point,' I said, 'but Attlee was a politician. He was prime minister in the 1940s.'

'Way back in olden times,' he said. 'Like Shakespeare.'

'Not as olden as Shakespeare,' I said.

'Oh?' he said, and went away, satisfied.

Imelda was looking pale and tired from the sleepless nights, but whenever the baby was quiet and content her spirits lifted. She still didn't quite believe that her child was a reincarnation and I didn't try to persuade her. Her belief or disbelief didn't affect the situation one way or another. But she did broach the subject with her health visitor and that proved unwise. The health visitor was out of her depth and didn't like it. She became defensive and almost hostile.

'Put such ideas right out of your head,' she told Imelda. 'Young mothers often get wild notions about their babies caused by stress and lack of sleep. See that your husband pulls his weight. Make him do his bit.'

Imelda was insulted by the suggestion that Raymond was not pulling his weight. She was as protective of him as she was of her baby. Besides, he was a most attentive father and could hardly be parted from little Clem. Imelda has a stubborn streak and the health visitor's attitude caused her to veer towards my opinion about the baby.

'What does she know about reincarnation anyway?' she said.

'A good question,' I said.

'For that matter, what do *you* know about reincarnation?' she said, for in her disbelieving moments she reproached me for having complicated her life.

'I keep an open mind,' I said, but of course that was not true. As far as little Clem was concerned, my mind was tightly shut.

We never found out for certain who leaked the story of the reincarnation of Clement Attlee to the press. Imelda blamed Mr Cranch; my mother suspected Psycho Dave; and Psycho Dave was convinced it was the health visitor. When I say it was leaked to the press I'm exaggerating slightly. There was just one item with a photograph and a cartoon in a single newspaper and a passing reference in a comment column in one of the Sundays. The other papers did not follow it up and television camera crews and the foreign press did not camp outside our door.

The reporter seemed a likeable chap, Imelda said. He gave her a bunch of chrysanthemums and maidenhair fern and said he was doing a survey on new babies. He said that those who participated would be entered in a draw for huge prizes that could secure the baby's future. He said that he wouldn't take up more than ten minutes of her time. Imelda consulted Raymond who happened to be at home and neither could see any harm in taking the chance to secure their baby's future, so they let the reporter and the photographer in. Imelda was impressed, too, that the photographer gave her a few minutes to change into a dress and put on some make-up. The reporter noted down all the details of their ages and occupations before he got on to the subject of reincarnation. Imelda says that as soon as he said the word she smelt a rat. She says that all she said when asked if she believed that the baby was the reincarnation of Clement Attlee was: 'What if he is?' and all Raymond said was: 'It's not a crime, is it?' She says that Raymond was magnificent and that he threatened to knock the reporter's block off if he didn't leave – a detail which I found hard to believe. The pair did leave and when the front door closed behind them the flap of the letterbox opened and an application form for a premium bond fell on to the mat. Imelda threw open the door, tore up the form and hurled it after the reporter.

'Our baby is Clem Attlee returned to earth' ran the subhead on the article the following day. We couldn't fault the photograph

– it was a lovely family group and, if her pride would have allowed, Imelda would have written off for copies.

The cartoon showed a reporter with a microphone interviewing a baby in a nappy and asking: 'Who's going to renationalise the choo-choos, then?'

There were rows in every room of the house that evening. My mother stalked up to Psycho Dave's room and accused him of shooting his mouth off about the baby in the pub so that the newspaper had got to hear about it. Psycho Dave swore it wasn't his fault and to emphasise his innocence he kicked in the door of his built-in wardrobe.

Imelda banged on Mr Cranch's door and accused him of alerting the press in retaliation for the baby's having given him sleep-disturbed nights. Mr Cranch was terrified of the anger of females and became so confused that he couldn't marshal any coherent defence. I had to intervene to save him for I was convinced that it was not Mr Cranch who had betrayed us. Psycho Dave maintained it was the health visitor because he had had some dealings with the social services on account of what they called his little loss of control episodes and this had left him with an aversion to anyone in the caring professions. The poor infant, bewildered by all this uproar, cried louder and longer that night and no one got a wink of sleep. After that, Imelda became embarrassed to go out of the house. She said people in the shops were whispering and giving her strange looks. She took to going everywhere by car and shopping at a supermarket miles away. She said she couldn't stand being treated like a nutter.

Then Mr Cranch gave notice that he was leaving. He said he was falling asleep at work because the baby kept him awake all night. He said he could have put up with that, but when it came to trying to raise from the dead politicians who had long since passed on and other spooky goings-on a line had to be drawn somewhere, so he'd gone to the council and put his case before them and they'd found him a little flat in a hard-to-let block which had the advantage of being near the warehouse where he worked. He said he was sorry to leave after being a resident for twenty years but that if he'd known in the beginning that things were going to get out of hand with people going in for voodoo and what not he never would have rented a room there in the first place.

It was shortly after this that the social worker began to pay regular calls. Her name was Marion and she was so full of friendliness that Imelda took against her from the start. She was a mum herself, Marion said, and she knew how stressful having a new baby was. Imelda said she was a grown woman and was perfectly capable of dealing with a bit of stress. Marion said that women were conditioned into not asking for help when they needed it. Imelda said that if she needed help she would simply go out on to the landing and shout and several members of her family would come to her aid right away. She offered to demonstrate this but Marion said that that would not be necessary. Marion said that after childbirth a woman's hormones ran riot and that this could result in her having all sorts of strange ideas about her baby. Imelda said that if the town hall cared to supply a list of permitted ideas she would try to adopt them.

She complained bitterly to us about the social worker and so it was unfortunate that Psycho Dave chose the time of one of Marion's visits to pop in to see his nephew. On hearing that Marion was from the social services he suffered another loss of control episode and, even though out of respect for Imelda and the baby he did not kick the door down, his outburst was vehement enough to cause Marion to remember that she had an urgent appointment elsewhere and take her leave. Imelda said that when she looked out of the window afterwards she could see the woman sitting in her car and scribbling furiously in her notebook.

Imelda and Ray told no one about their plans to go to Australia until they had made all the arrangements. It was only for a trial period, Imelda said, to see how they liked it and to give Ray's parents an opportunity to see their grandson. Ray's brother-in-law had his own building business and would give Ray a job and if they liked the life then maybe they would apply for permission to stay. If they didn't, well then they'd be more settled after having had a chance to see a bit of the world. In any case, she was fed up of being spied upon. It was her belief, she said, that the social workers in the municipal hall had a file as long as your arm about herself and Ray and the baby. 'I won't stand for it,' Imelda said.

My mother was furious and blamed me, and was only slightly mollified when I offered her a return air ticket to Melbourne so that she could spend Christmas with Imelda and Ray and little Clem. Psycho Dave was devastated, but on this occasion did not kick down a door, which Raymond now as a sign of progress. 'You see!' Ray said to me. 'He's growing out of it.' Ray made me promise to be a brother to Psycho Dave and, although I had managed without a brother for all these years and Dave might not have been the one I would have chosen, I agreed.

We were all very depressed for a few weeks after Imelda and Ray and little Clem flew off from Heathrow. Their letters and postcards, telling us how much they were enjoying the sunshine and the space and how well the baby had settled down, were no consolation. I think it was the silence in the house that made me realise what had happened. It seemed like a great empty shell, a vacuum waiting to be filled.

I consulted with my new brother, Psycho Dave, and we made our plans. 'It's a window of opportunity,' I told him, a phrase that so impressed him that he repeated it every time we talked. We finished the jobs we had in hand and refused any further offers and went to work full time on converting the house into flats.

Psycho Dave could do anything with his hands and kept on working each day until I told him to stop. The first flat we completed was the one that included Mr Cranch's old room. It sold in a matter of weeks. People loved the high ceilings and the big bay window that was almost a room in itself. And that sale brought in enough money to pay for the other conversions. Now we are completing the last – my mother's big garden flat. Psycho Dave has taken a room with her. She has become a mother to him. He is unfailingly respectful and helpful with the chores. Sometimes I think she prefers him to me. He seldom kicks down a door now and in any case I took the precaution of fitting ball-bearing closers instead of locks to my mother's internal doors so that even if he kicks one of them it merely springs open and any damage to the paintwork can easily be repaired with a dab of Dulux. It reduces privacy somewhat but, as with so much in life, damage limitation is the best that can be hoped for.

I have a fine flat on the ground floor and the other three flats are ready to be put on the market. There will be enough money for Imelda and Ray to buy a house in Melbourne and for my mother to fly back and forth to spend the cold months of the year with them. She will have summer all the year round. She can buy a small house out there if she wants. She doesn't need to work in the dry-cleaners any more.

My father's wishes have been fulfilled. The house he bought to secure his family's future has done its job. He would be content.

Imelda often sends us photographs of little Clem. He is developing and changing fast, no longer the little baby I remember. Sometimes when I look at the photographs I have my doubts. I wonder if the feelings I had when I first saw him lying in his milk crate could have been mistaken. But then I remember how strong was my conviction and I think of what he has already achieved. When he was born, our lives were circumscribed; we were imprisoned in that large house, unable to use it to fulfil our desires. Now we are free and secure. Little Clem has seen to that. No ordinary baby could have accomplished so much.

I keep an eye out for news items about Australia – everything from cricket scores to changes in the government. When I'm in Earls Court I pick up the free Australian newspapers and read about whatever is the topic of the day: the mining industry in New South Wales, the prospect of republicanism, relations with the Pacific Rim. I know little Clem is at work, in his quiet, indirect and subtle way, moving here, shaking there, causing things to happen.

Slugs and Snails | Ros Barber

Tabloids still call me 'the slug girl'. For twenty years they have slung my tag mercilessly into the public colosseum, contorting each life-turn of significance into headline puns and thumb decisions. Moments that in my peers would pass unnoticed blast across the country in alliterative feasts. Complete strangers know of my grades, my operations, my favourite films. Trials and triumphs alike are trumpeted from news-stand to corner shop. My marriage to Peter, a man who had achieved many things besides his PhD on arachnids, became 'Slug Girl Weds Spider Man'. For my tiny, too early, translucent daughters, the papers sang 'Twin Lady Bugs Bring Slug Girl Joy'. When Ellie died, the press poured into my life like water through a holed hull. 'Slug Mum!' they shouted, crushing their colleagues for quotes. I was sinking, and all they could do was add their weight.

I was their childhood sweetheart, their favourite story of 1978. Susan, nine, found starving in the cellar of the family home. The bright little girl in the picture whose father had not been seen since early September. The plucky and talented youngster, who recently starred in her school's production of *Joseph and his*

Amazing Technicolor Dreamcoat and had survived an astonishing four weeks by sucking rainwater from the bricks and eating slugs. There were other elements to my cellar diet, never adopted as nicknames. I might have been 'mouse-dropping girl' or 'cockroach girl' or 'urine girl'. But *any* monicker was rancid meat to a starving dog.

For the next seven years, I was known to my peers as Slimy. They circled me as I shrank into the cracks between the kerbstones.

'What do they taste like?' they shouted.

My tongue remembered the slippery leather, metallic. I found slugs in my plimsolls, my inkwell, my Thermos flask; tucked into my sandwiches, my PE shorts; dangled in my hair. They made clay slugs in art lessons and threw them at me in the break.

Though I grew tall and lean, my hair thread mercury, my features fine, I was loveless in a fifth form bulging with dark fumblings and used condoms. Not even mathematical whiz-kids would integrate with Slimy the Slug Girl. The gobbing, smoking punks I met in the precinct, happy to stroke my anonymous buttocks through leather jeans, learnt quickly of my name and steered north. I longed to be invisible, to slip between them like an ether they could sense but had no name for. To haunt them like the screw they never had. To quiver their hedgehog hair, slip into the slits of their pinned jeans and stiffen them until they begged for mercy. But for now I would peer through the sweater rack of C&A, watch them scuff their Docs and, with women hanging off their belts, taunt grannies and grind butts into the flower-beds.

On my seventeenth birthday, my aunt's pink bathroom shag pile sucked up two pints of blood before our neighbour kicked the door down. It was no cry for help, more of an exit visa. When I rose through the fog I found my aunt screaming at me – all she had done for me, be so stupid, everything to live for, could I be thinking of, daughter to her, should have said something. When I was crammed with stolen blood, the hospital shrink tried to scare me. He took me to see a girl my age rolling her eyes and crapping in a bag because they'd saved her body but not her brain. I was under surveillance now – the bathroom lock was removed and I slept on a camp-bed in my aunt's room. When she went out she left me with Laurie next door.

Laurie was a widower who had retired from the fire service with bad health. He was a hero who had saved many lives, diving into fires with inadequate gear to haul out unconscious children. His lungs were wrecked with the smoke and he wheezed as he lowered and raised his scarred body, piercing mine, smothering my mouth with his dry and breathless-blue lips. And my aunt would come back from her ceramics class and collect her sore and smiling niece, thanking the man whose semen was still swimming inside me. I seemed so content, she let me have my own room again.

There were things I wouldn't do for Laurie. Because I was vegetarian, I said, and he laughed his black, smoky laugh and pushed me towards his flies before I bucked away. I couldn't stand anything fleshy in my mouth. Not just meat, but bananas, boiled carrots, cheese, even toast if it wasn't cooked twice to get it crisp right through. It came alive in my mouth, crawled in the channel between my lips and gums. Sometimes if I ate something and it got slimy in my stomach, I had to throw up. I threw up a lot, and then my stomach started cramping. One night at Laurie's I was submerged in pain. He took me upstairs to his bed and lay beside me, stroking the hair from my face while I sweated and cried. I said I had to go to the toilet but he said I didn't. His wife had been just the same, he said, and I was going to be all right.

Laurie wrapped the baby in a blanket and took it downstairs, with all the other stuff that came out of me. I didn't care about anything except that the pain was gone. The ceiling was dotted with tiny blue flowers that his wife must have chosen and the dead woman's sheets were soaked with my blood. The baby crackled its peculiar newborn cry downstairs; a police car shrilled in the distance; a boy yelled for his dog in the street. Then Laurie came up with tears lighting his face and said that the baby was dead. He helped me to the chair where his old uniform was neatly draped and I watched as he bundled the bedclothes into a bin bag. He turned the mattress over and his fireman's muscles stood proud under the silver hairs.

Later I watched him from my window, wheezing as he dug beside the hydrangeas. The bare spot on his skull glowed like polished pewter in the moonlight. Rain began to fall; stricken orbs smashing themselves against the sill. The spade chucked into the clay, and steam lifted from Laurie's glittering head. Exhausted, he looked up to my window, seeing nothing. At last I was invisible, trembling on the edges of existence. I watched him bury our baby, the darkness enveloping us both.

I was too scared to see Laurie after that, and he was too

scared to see me. My aunt was angry. What had I done to upset Mr Crest? In late summer Laurie's hydrangeas, previously pink, bloomed half blue, half pale, chemically altered by the body beneath. From the cobalt mopheads I imagined my baby a boy. One evening, while the swallows were looping and screeching over the aerials and the first breaths of autumn were coaxing the beech into copper, I must have decided to join him. Though I woke in casts and pulleys, I swear to this day I don't remember falling.

My return was greeted with window locks and the camp-bed back on the floor next to my aunt's exuberant queen-size. She had cancelled her classes, and forced me to follow her from room to room. When she had to go to the bathroom she had me sit on the linen basket with my back turned like a makeshift confessional priest. She told me plainly I had stolen her life and I only wished she would let me steal my own. But there is more than one way to kill yourself, and finally I chose the method my father had chosen for me. Already slender and armed with a passionate abhorrence of food, I found it no harder than letting out breath. My aunt ignored me. Then she pleaded, shouted, blackmailed and finally despaired.

Two weeks before my eighteenth birthday I was sent to the Elizabeth Morgan Centre for Eating Disorders. The girls there had more bones sticking out of them than a desecrated graveyard. Their eyes were large in their skulls, like puppies drowning. Food was served four times a day and taken away without comment. Our punishment was talk.

The mistress of the house, Jennifer Morgan, was a reptilian

goddess spitting fire into the tinder of our self-hatred. Her husband Felix, however, was wild and delightful. Their daughter's death had not scaled him the way it had his lizardy wife – he was soft-skinned and warm-blooded, with open ears rather than her closed spiracles. His legs splayed across the linoleum were the cue for my life story, slugs and Laurie and all. He wept like a saint as I let him find my little rotting boy in Laurie's garden. He told me I had become not a slug, but a snail, protecting my jellied organs in an uncrackable shell. And he took me in his arms to water my cheeks with his tears.

The delicious Felix and I made a deal. I would learn to love food and he would learn to love me, for though he liked his women without scales, he preferred a little more meat on them. We took it slowly, conquering fruit by stages. He described to me in six hundred words the erotic tease of juice exploding on the tongue. We soldiered on to other foods. The girl I shared a room with died part-way through dairy products. I took it as a cue to make my move.

Felix was rough in my mouth, his giant tongue stiff and unsluglike. He was salivating uncontrollably, his lips drenching my chin. Something urgent pushed out the waistband of his corduroys. He was tearing open the sleeve of a condom, rolling it on to his unzipped shaft, when that shaft sank with a knock at the door. I slithered back to my chair as he recovered.

'You seem to be cured,' said the lizard, her tongue flicking. 'You are being discharged.'

And so it was that I returned to my aunt's with an unsurpassed passion for fucking and food, and found an unclothed, white fleshed man asleep on my bed, his arm curled over my pillow.

'Thank you, God,' I sighed, and lay down beside him. I ran a finger over his bony hip. The August air hung in heavy folds around us, pressing pearls of perspiration from his temple. I blew softly on his forehead, cooling him, flickering his eyes awake.

Startled, he rolled away from me and dropped on to the floor, crouching like a leopard. I laughed.

'What are you doing on my bed?'

'Oh God,' he said, 'it's you.' No longer scared, he gathered the sheet around his waist and sat beside me. 'What are you doing back?'

'Discharged,' I said. 'Where's your mother?'

'Shopping,' he said. 'She's managed a lot of that since you were incarcerated.'

'Well, we'll have to put a stop to that,' I said. 'You still haven't told me what you're doing on my bed.'

'Sleeping.'

I went to jab him in the side.

'All right! Mum said I could use your room while you were away. I've come to stay for a while. She's got her pottery stuff set up in my old room.'

'What's the matter? Get kicked out?'

'No, I've finished my doctorate. I'm looking for a job. I thought I might look closer to home.'

'Good!' I said, flouncing out. 'I'll just go and find myself a bed-sit.'

'No!' he laughed, running, clutching the sheet with one hand

and catching me with the other. 'Stay here, you loony. I've missed you.'

'Thanks, Cuz.'

'I'll sleep on the floor in here,' he said. 'I'll get my old mattress down from the loft.'

'Great,' I said. 'Terminal snoring.'

My aunt was happier now that Peter was home and felt safe to leave him to look after me. He didn't seem to be trying to find a job at all, but we played gin rummy, Monopoly and beat your neighbour. At lunchtime we would compete to make ridiculous sandwiches, like cheese, marmalade and anchovy, or rum butter, cornflakes and pickled onions. He thought it was funny I could eat so much now without being sick. I said there were still a few things I wouldn't eat. And then one night, as I tuned to his tidal breathing ebbing and flowing across the floor – as I floated into sleep – he suddenly said, 'Why did your dad do it, do you think?'

'I don't know,' I murmured. 'How would I know?'

'I do,' he said quietly. 'I've known for years. Do you want to?'

'I'm not sure I do,' I said.

'Well I'll tell you a story. You can stop me if you want.' Peter propped himself on one elbow.

Once upon a time, he said, there was a happy family. A mummy, a daddy, and two little children. A boy and a girl.

'I didn't have a brother,' I interrupted.

'Shut up,' he said. 'I'll get to that later.'

Well, the family seemed happy, but the mummy didn't want to be with the daddy at night, so when the house was quiet and dark he would visit one of the other bedrooms. Sometimes the little girl's, and sometimes the little boy's.

'This is boring,' I said. 'It's got nothing to do with me.'

'I'll skip a few years.'

The little boy grew up and decided he would become a doctor. That way he could make everyone else better, even if he would never be better himself. He was very popular with his patients and in the community, and everyone thought of him as a good man. He got married to a beautiful woman who bore him a daughter, and he felt he had never been happier in his life.

'And then his wife died,' I said.

'Yes, she did.'

His daughter began to grow up, and although she was still a little girl, her face took on some of her dead mother's softness and colour, and when her father looked into her eyes it was as though his lover's soul were looking back at him. He was frightened. He was drawn to his daughter and feared that his love for her might cease to be fatherly. He told his fears to his sister, but she would not take them seriously, believing it to be nothing more than the stress of his grief. He'd worked so hard at being good, at being different from his father, and now his daughter's beauty was undermining him. He burned with the legacy of his own father's visits and could not let the pain seep down through the generations. He had to put a stop to it. And because he loved his daughter, he couldn't actually kill her. The most he could do was leave her there to die.

For a while there was no other sound in the room but breathing.

'But why did he try to kill her? Why didn't he kill himself?' I said.

'He could prevent more pain that way.'

'How do you know? He didn't tell that to your mother.'

'I've thought about it a lot, Susan. He thought you and your children and their children in turn might have to suffer as he did. He wanted to stop that. It's the only thing that makes sense.'

'And you're qualified, are you?'

'I've studied why creatures do what they do.'

'Oh piss off, Peter, you studied insects, not psychology.'

'Spiders.'

'Spiders then. You're not bloody Freud, anyway.'

'You know what I think, Susie?'

'I don't care.'

'You know what I think, cousin? You're afraid he was right.'

My eyes began to sting and I wiped my nose on the back of my hand. He shuffled his sleeping bag across the floor like a pupating caterpillar.

'I agree with him on one thing,' he said.

'What's that?' I sniffed.

'You *are* beautiful.'

He leant forward and touched his lips on mine – a brief taste of toothpaste.

'That's a joke,' I said.

'A joke is sleeping feet apart in the same room,' he said. 'This is serious.'

He shed his sleeping bag and climbed in beside me. Velvety skin and bristly hairs.

'Is this all right?' I asked.

'Of course,' he said. 'You're not my sister. You're just my cousin.'

We married in October, with trees shedding their confetti. My aunt wept for the daughter-in-law she might have had. But as always, it seemed, she had me. I soon fell pregnant and swelled rapidly through the spring, stuffing my unborn with *aubergines au gratin* and *moules marinières*. The ultrasound showed two tiny hearts twitching like tadpoles still trapped in their spawn. Two piano-key spines, two skulls haunting the camera.

Three months too early, I felt a pop in Marks and Spencer and flooded the lingerie department. The babies were frail and had to be cut out of me. They placed a screen across my chest, and Peter squeezed my hand and watched intently. I felt rummaging, tugging, but not the pain of before. My two struggling daughters, their paper-thin skins like Chinese lanterns, were again carried away from my sight. By the time I was wheeled to the Baby Unit, they were splayed out like frogs for dissection, sedated to block their resistance to cannulas, sensors and wires. I sat between them, hour on hour, mesmerised by the blipping of their monitors. On the fifth day I woke at dawn, washed up on a current of panic. I cried for the night staff to take me to Special Care. As I arrived a knot of nurses unwound and froze. Ellie was already dead.

Cassie fought on. I pumped out the milk that came flooding

to save her. At four weeks old, still tiny and wired, they let me put her to my breast. Her mouth came to rest on my skin like the Holy Grail. She grew in strength and suck from week to week, and finally, on the day she should have been born, we took her home.

Peter threw his love on to Cassie; but I was snagged on Ellie. She was overlooked in all the joy. It grated for my aunt to say, 'Well, you've got one beautiful baby.' Ellie was discarded, the packaging that little Cassie came with. I started to sink. I was going to Ellie, and knew that Cassie couldn't be left behind. I cuddled her close to me and whispered lullabies. In the morning, Peter found Cassie bluer than Wedgwood. He sobbed until my aunt called the police.

Soon, a tent went up in next-door's garden. The papers sucked the blood out of my trial. Peter, white and crumbling, sat alone. His mother, and Felix Morgan, testified to my instability. My counsel would not let me take the stand. And Laurie, now remarried to a turkey-necked woman in pearls, also gave evidence. Whispered about his daughter, also smothered. How he had, misguidedly, protected me. The jury winced at a Polaroid of bones beside the hydrangeas.

Once again I'm locked in, though the food is a little more traditional. There's light this time, and company, and water that tastes not of London brick, but chlorine. Peter is standing by me, and sends me longing letters twice a week. At his visits, we discuss in whispers the bedroom act that will mark my recovery. Sometimes we cry into each other's fingers for the twins. And sometimes, as I lie on my bunk after lock-in and listen to the despairing shouts of my sisters, I believe I am finally sane. Having come so far I may even, at last, eat snails. They no longer seem to share the vileness of their hideously unhoused relations. Felix once said that the slug craves the snail's containment whilst the snail envies the confident ugliness of the slug. Although I now accept that confident ugliness saved my life, I am not prepared to revisit and savour my saviour. But I am, I believe, ready to eat its cousin.

Chapter
3

When we get home from school we take off our coats and run through the dark house, shouting for her. She is standing in the middle of the living-room, like a sentinel. Wrapped round her head is a towel, which entirely covers her face. Both her arms are stretched out towards us, with their palms turned up. She seems to be offering us something. I almost run into them, to be hugged. The left-hand side of her body flickers with blue light from the television screen. Before we can do anything, before we can understand what has happened, she begins to speak, but her voice is almost drowned by the plaintive voice of Ryan O'Neal. It's *Peyton Place*, after the accident. He's still in hospital, crippled, maybe for life. I can't help myself, I turn and look at the screen. Ryan is hoisting himself up on a bar, suspended above the bed. His brother is standing beside him, anxious, listening to what the doctors are about to say. I look back towards my mother. She tells us not to worry, her voice oddly toneless, muffled by the towel, and to call an ambulance at once. I edge past her and sit down on the sofa, shaking, surprised by my fear, my satchel clutched to my chest. We hear Titus bark suddenly, outside, from beneath the window. My sister runs over to the phone and dials 999.

My mother is quite still, standing beside the window with her head turned slightly towards the outside, as though she's watching someone walk down the empty hill opposite the house. Sitting behind her, I see her towel-swathed head silhouetted against the heavy drizzle of the early-evening sky. I wonder what's happened to her face but I'm afraid to ask, suddenly remembering a film I saw where there's nothing beneath the bandage, or was it a mask? Nothing but the ivory smoothness of an egg. Together, we listen to Alice explain how to reach the house. Her voice gets sharper as she tells them when to turn off the road. She describes the track leading down to the valley, the house behind the double gate, the mountain ash by the door, and as I listen it all seems new. I wonder how anyone could live there. I turn my head slightly, so that my mother is no longer at the centre of my vision, and see how the tree outside is blurred by rain, by low cloud. I stare out into the water-filled air. Finally, when I am calm, I ask my mother what has happened. She starts, as though she has forgotten that I am there. She turns her head in what she must feel is the direction of my voice and begins to speak. But she miscalculates by half a yard. Sickened with fear, as though I am lost, I move to the left, so that I am sitting where she seems to expect me to be.

'It was so silly,' she says. 'I was going to do some chips for your tea and I thought I'd better change the oil in the pan. So I opened the stove door and threw the oil in and there was a sort of explosion. I didn't realise what I'd done at first. Then my face felt so hot I went to look at myself in the mirror and I couldn't even see where I was going because there was something wrong with my glasses. So I took them off and saw myself. I was all red! I almost laughed, but it hurt to move. Then it all began to burn so I splashed it with cold water.' She pauses. 'What an idiotic thing to do,' she says wonderingly, as if to herself, while I nod, unseen. Then, with a short laugh, she adds: 'What on earth will your father say?'

By the time the ambulance arrives she is crouched at the foot of the stairs with Alice and me beside her. She has begun to cry, rubbing the towel against her hidden face, against where her eyes must be, to dry them. Alice reaches up and puts an arm round her shoulder. When we hear the ambulance coming down the track she gestures to me to open the door and helps our mother to her feet. The strangest thing, I think, as I watch her move sightlessly across the hall, is that she has covered her eyes with the towel. Perhaps she doesn't want to see herself any more. Or maybe it's us she doesn't want to see.

They stumble together towards the open door, where the ambulance driver is waiting. I flutter round them, taking my mother's coat from the rack, knocking my father's cap on to the floor, picking it up and dropping the coat. As soon as my mother is in the grasp of the ambulance driver Alice comes back. She doesn't even look at me. She picks up the coat and carries it to my mother, who has turned towards us. She seems to have stopped crying, although there are two damp patches, like stains, on the towel. The towel has rows of brightly coloured fish on a

71

sea-blue background. Little bubbles come out of their mouths to form a border. She has wrapped the towel around her head the way she knots it after washing her hair. It looks like a turban that has slipped down over her face. I suddenly want to laugh. She looks ridiculous. But then I am frightened again. I wonder what her face is like. Perhaps it has all been burnt away. Perhaps there is nothing left except her eyes. I stand there with my mouth open, imagining my mother's head as a skull with open sockets, alive and staring eyes, like Boris Karloff in *The Mummy*. Alice glances up at me impatiently, then takes my arm and pulls herself close. The ambulance driver is leading our mother up the path beside the house. The ambulance drives off into the mist. As we close the door, I can hear the credits of *Peyton Place* from the living-room.

My father brings her back from hospital later that evening. The burns are superficial but they have a curious effect on the way she looks. Her eyebrows and eyelashes have been singed off, along with the first inch of her hair. She has a bright red line around the top of her face, like the rubber ring used to seal preserves. She looks naked, with her eyes startled open and exposed. Her skin is shiny, scarlet, with blistering on her nose and cheeks. She reminds me of one of those glossy school exercise books left out in the sun. When she smiles her teeth are oddly white. The first thing she does when she sees us is smile.

'My poor darlings,' she says. 'You must have been so worried.'

Our father helps her take off her coat. We stand and stare.

'And how do you think I felt?' he says to her, ignoring us. 'They didn't even know which hospital you'd been taken to.' She lowers her arms for him. The coat slides off.

We stare as though we have never seen her before, and she stares back. She seems to be hurt, but also irritated, by our blank open-mouthed expressions, half-unnerved, half-curious. Then she looks at us as though we are equally strange to her, as though she sees us through new eyes, as if a layer of skin has been burnt off her vision, or off the world. Her smile comes back.

'Look,' she says, opening her bag. 'They've given me this spray for my face. To kill the pain. It looks like lacquer.'

'Does it hurt?' I ask.

'Of course it hurts,' my father says sharply.

Alice runs across and hugs her, impulsively and with unexpected violence, so that she almost staggers back against the door. I wonder why I don't run across as well, merely watching while she strokes her daughter's hair away from her face and smiles down at her. But the smile hurts her cheeks and she lets it fade away, and I am glad. Alice clings to her waist. When she finally lets go it is with a little shrug of her shoulders. Mum seems upset. She reaches out but Alice has gone back to her chair beside the fire; she sits down, humming a little tune.

'Aren't you going to make your mother a cup of tea?' Dad says. I go into the kitchen.

That night our parents argue. We are fast asleep in the next room, but we wake up when we hear their voices. Although we say nothing to each other – we never do – we know that we are both awake, both listening. Our parents are arguing in the usual way. Her voice is low and tearful. It's difficult to hear what she's saying. He is shouting. It is obvious from his tone, as well as from his words, that they are arguing in circles. Finally, she begins to cry more loudly. He stops talking. He goes into the bathroom, slamming both doors behind him, and we breathe out together, relieved. After some time he goes back to the bedroom and starts to shout again. This time her voice is raised as well. Nobody understands her, she says. Nobody knows what it's like to live there day after day, alone, afraid of the emptiness, waiting for you to come home. And when you do, your silence, as though the house's muteness infected you. She feels like screaming, she says. She stands at the window and stares out into the emptiness of the fields and feels like screaming and screaming until somebody hears her.

We lie in the next room, listening.

When we come home from school the next day she is watching television. She has Titus on her lap; she is stroking him in a distracted, mechanical way. There is salad in the fridge, she says. When we look at her, she reacts impatiently.

'I'm not a freak, you know.'

Alice throws down her satchel and goes upstairs to change. When she comes down she is wearing jeans and her hair is stuffed up into a knitted hat. She runs out of the house without speaking. We see her a few moments later on the slope of the hill outside. She is jumping up and down as though trying to catch something. Then, with a spurt, she disappears into the mist.

'I don't know what she finds to do,' Mum says. 'I worry about her here. I worry about you both.' Her hand goes up to her face and strokes her cheek. 'I saw a monster once,' she says. 'During the war. I was waiting for the bus in Queen Street. It was during black-out, all the streetlights were turned off, you could hardly see the bus. Then a great long car, a limousine I suppose it must have been, slowed down in front of us. I was with Barbara, we must have just finished work. And when the car stopped we saw that there were curtains at all the windows, except for the windscreen, which was smoked glass or something. I remember it was cold, and we were all so tired and sick of the war I just felt angry. I wanted to see who'd drive around in luxury like that when we were all on rations. So I pressed my face up against the glass and there was a crack in the curtain and I looked inside.' She pauses. 'And there was a man inside, with a dinner jacket and a bow tie, and the head of a pig. I saw him and screamed, I'll never forget it, and he turned to look at me, and his face was so sad I suddenly stopped screaming and started to cry. I didn't know the face of an animal could be so sad. But of course, he wasn't an animal at all.' She lets her hand fall down into her lap. 'Barbara caught a glimpse of him as well, otherwise no one would ever have believed me. I don't think I'd have believed it myself.'

I sit down beside my mother and stroke the dog, who twists until his pink-white belly faces up. Mum grabs the dog suddenly and thrusts his face into hers.

'You silly little thing,' she cries. She turns to me.

'I'm sorry it's only salad,' she says. 'I just couldn't bear the idea of cooking.'

She looks at me as I take the dog from her and hold it against my chest. It wriggles to be put down.

'Haven't you got any homework?' she says. I am watching television. Dorothy Malone is walking across the square, beside the bandstand, in a striped dress. She looks worried. She doesn't know that she is being followed. We watch her turn towards the shop, enthralled.

'I'll do it later,' I say, going into the kitchen to get my salad. I bring it into the living-room and eat it on my lap. We are back in the hospital. Ryan O'Neal is sitting up in bed, without his T-shirt. By the time my sister gets back I've finished eating and the final music has begun. My mother tells her what's happened but she doesn't care.

Her face is flushed. She pulls off her hat and her hair falls into her eyes. It has started raining. She shakes her head like a dog.

That evening she begins to imitate me. We are sitting beside each other on the sofa and at first I don't notice. It's only when I scratch my cheek and see that she is scratching her cheek too that I become aware of what she is doing. I realise that she has been copying me for some time. I turn to face her angrily and see that she is mimicking my anger. Her face is twisted up in rage.

'What are you doing?' I say.

'What are you doing?' she says.

I pick up a book from beside the sofa and pretend to read. Alice reaches down and picks up her pantomime book. I cross my legs, and see her cross her legs in an exaggerated way. I brush my hair back off my face and see her hand move up towards her head. I turn towards her and hiss: 'Stop it!'

'Stop it,' she says in a quiet, satisfied voice.

'For God's sake, leave me alone!' I cry.

'For God's sake, leave me alone.'

My hand lashes out and slaps her arm. It leaves a vivid red mark, like a scald. She looks at me coldly for a moment and then slaps my arm with all her force. We stare at each other, like cats, until I feel tears prickling behind my eyes and turn away. It occurs to me that if I refuse to look at her, she won't be allowed to look at me. The nature of the game will force her to stop. I turn to face the wall.

But Alice has invented the game. She pulls my hair. When I hit her a second time our mother shouts at us to stop, her face an angry red beneath the livid burns. She tells me that there is nothing more despicable than to hit a girl.

'But she hit me first,' I plead.

'Aren't you old enough to defend yourself?' she says.

'I didn't,' Alice says.

'I think your father'll be having a word with both of you when he gets back from the pub.'

I go into the kitchen to make some tea.

As I wait for the kettle to boil I stare through the window into the night. It has stopped raining and the mist has lifted. Moonlight touches the branches of the tree and the sharp edge of the hill beyond. Slowly, as I look through the window, the furrows and creases of the land emerge from the dark. A single house-light flickers on and then off, as though someone has entered a room and then changed his mind. I wonder whose farm it is. It is hard to judge distances, hard to know how far the light has carried. The stars, for example, are very far away. I rest my elbows on the window sill and stare up into the sky. The light of the moon is reflected, I think. A great dead lump of stone that picks up the light of the sun and flings it out again, but changed. I wonder if the earth reflects the light as well, and who will see it. And will it be the same light, or different. Waiting for the water to boil, I imagine the universe as a string of dulled grey mirrors, picking up the light and passing it on, distorted. Like Chinese whispers. Perhaps the only way to keep the message alive would be to make it simple.

Then I see the double beam of headlights swing up from the dark, from behind the brow of the hill. It must be my father's car, I think.

That night, in bed, when Alice says 'Goodnight', I refuse to answer. Even when she starts crying and begs me to speak, I refuse to say 'Goodnight'.

'How can you be so cruel?' she says through her tears.

I want to tell her that she has been cruel to me, and that the game of imitation scares me. But that would mean speaking and I haven't forgiven her yet. It is only when I hear our parents getting ready for bed and think they might come in to say goodnight that I finally relent. I am scared they will find her crying.

'Goodnight,' I say.

'Oh, thank you,' she says.

A few minutes later we hear them talking in strained, low voices. I have the strangest feeling they are planning to take us into the woods and leave us there, the way Hansel and Gretel's parents did. I shall fill my pockets with stones, I think. I shall take my sister with me, wherever I go. I am suddenly filled with love for her. I reach across and feel for her hand. There is no more noise from our parents' room. They must be asleep, too exhausted to argue any longer.

Our mother is too embarrassed to go shopping this weekend. She says that everyone will look at her scarlet face with its rubbery skin and naked staring eyes. But when we get back from town and I carry the box of groceries into the kitchen, calling 'Mum', there's no reply. I put down the box and see a letter on the table, beside the stove. I am about to hide it, I don't know why, when my father comes up behind me and takes it from my hand.

He tells us to unpack the groceries and says that he will soon be back. We pretend to be adults, make sandwiches for lunch, nervously excited to be alone. It is like a game and it is serious as well, as we test our freedom. In the afternoon the car comes down the track and our parents walk into the house together. It's hard to tell from our mother's injured face whether she has been crying or not. Our father is cautious with her, taking her coat and making her tea. She sits down at the kitchen table without speaking. When we move up towards her, Alice first, then me, she tries to hug us both. But we are wary. We shift away from her slightly. She leans forward then, and folds us in to her. She whispers in our ears that she loves us. She couldn't bear to lose us.

It took her face a long time to heal. First the blistered skin came off, revealing a fresh new surface that seemed almost false. She joked that it was like having her face peeled. How much younger she looked! We laughed. We were pleased to see that she was happy.

Slowly her eyebrows and eyelashes grew back, and the fringe of hair around her forehead. When it had grown beyond the bristly stage she went to have her hair cut, short, like the hair of a girl.

It wasn't until there was no trace at all of the accident left upon her face that she took the oil and, more carefully this time, poured it around the kitchen, and opened the windows to create a draught, and flung the bottle into the stove, and ran.

An Angel Passing Through | Judi Moore

It had not been a good day. The whole town was seething with people because of the Games and the heat and humidity had been fierce. The bar was a haven, of sorts. There was a big screen showing events from the Games but it was, mercifully, in back away from the bar itself. I could hear the occasional roars when an American did something clever, or missed doing something clever. I couldn't have cared less. I was on to my second beer, and blessing the air-conditioning, and waiting for Marianne.

Marianne was late. She was often late. She was often very late indeed – like by days. However, I was giving her more time than I usually did to fail to turn up because I knew the traffic would be dreadful, and she had to come across town. We were meeting in Scarlett's Bar, which was just about a block from where I worked, because we had thought it would be less difficult for her to get into town than for me to get out – so I had come straight from work. I felt grubby with the sticky heat and the street dirt and wanted a shower badly. I decided that if she didn't come in the next five minutes I would start for home. There was no logical reason to suppose that the day was going to improve. I might as well get a pizza on the way, and then a shower, and then an early night. I finished my beer.

The door opened and I looked round, sort of hoping it might be Marianne, but now almost settled on the pizza and shower plan. It wasn't Marianne, but I didn't turn back to the bar. It was a man. He was wearing one of those sad grey tracksuits that joggers and winos have, and he looked unsure of himself. But it was the head sticking out of that saggy tracksuit that held my attention. It was astonishingly beautiful – the head of an angel. And in the shadow inside the bar his eyes were lightest blue in sockets rimmed with indigo. He looked like a very tired angel.

He stopped just inside the door, apparently uncertain whether to come in or not. He was looking around, and, although I knew I was staring, I just couldn't take my eyes off him. He was very blond, with the hair cropped short, his face pale and those deep violet circles round his eyes.

I was still staring when he noticed. He started over towards me. I immediately regretted my curiosity. I knew, finally, that Marianne wasn't coming – wouldn't help me shift this unwelcome company. And I knew that he felt my face had been the one friendly thing in the bar, and that my glass was invitingly empty. Shit.

Quickly I turned back to the bar and gave my whole attention to my empty glass, while watching his approach in the mirror behind it. While I was at it I couldn't help noticing that my hair was completely deflated with the heat and hung in rats' tails and that my make-up – what there was of it – looked as if it hadn't been touched since I put it on this morning, which it hadn't.

Double shit. I don't go along with the theory that men won't make a pass if you look like hell. I don't like to look like hell – I like to look like me. The me in the mirror looked raddled. I sighed.

He finished up just beyond the stool next to mine at the bar. At least he had some manners, hadn't plunged immediately inside my personal space. He made no pretence, however, at having just ended up near me. He hadn't taken his eyes off me yet. He wasn't wasting any time, either.

'Hello,' he said, carefully. 'You drink with me. I score very good.'

That got me riled for a start. I hate the testosterone types who think that sex is a war and assume they're going to win every battle.

His English wasn't good. He hadn't lived here long. It sounded East European to me, as much as I know. I began to think that perhaps he didn't have a green card but had got some casual work nearby. That would explain his caution at the door. Closer to he had a dangerous look to him – exhausted, but sharp under that. If he hadn't been so tired I might have been in trouble, but as it was . . .

I had a choice. I could tell him to go screw himself and hope the barman would throw him out if he didn't like it, or I could accept the drink. I did hesitate, but not for long. His light-blue eyes turned out, close up, to have a wonderful dark rim to the irises. The deep shadows around them made him look vulnerable – and I was curious.

'OK,' I said. 'I'll have a beer with you, but you haven't scored.'

He smiled and said nothing. He ordered the beers by holding up two fingers in the old war-time sign for victory and saying something that sounded like a foreign variant of 'beer'. He didn't say please or thank you, but added a smile. The smile made him look more like an angel than ever. He had very good teeth. The barman smiled back.

The angel turned to me, with the gesture still in his fingers, and said it again, still with the angelic smile.

'I score very good. Yes.'

I held up two fingers in the same gesture. I said, 'You score – no.'

I pulled my fingers slowly down to make a fist. His smile faltered. Our beer came. He held out a handful of money to the barman, who took the price of the beer, showed him what he'd taken, and put it in the till. I began to wonder whether he lived here at all. Perhaps he had come for the Games? To cheer his people on? Perhaps he was a soldier? Perhaps he was a spy. Perhaps I should have slid off my bar stool and out the door before things had gotten this far.

He sat down on the stool he had been standing behind. That, somehow, gave the situation a reality it hadn't had before. I now had to entertain for my drink and I realised that was going to be really difficult. He didn't seem to have much English at all. I hadn't had much experience of being picked up by foreigners – hell, I'd never even had a holiday outside the States. I realised I didn't know what to do. His eyes never left my face. All I could do was smile. That was rewarding, because his own smile reappeared and I felt much happier dealing with an angel than with a man who might be a spy, or an illegal immigrant or – well, anything really.

We sat in silence for a while, and drank our beer. He shared his attention between my face and the big screen at the back of the bar. Occasionally he would point and nod. Although I had no interest in the Games I shifted in my seat so that I could see what he was pointing and nodding at. It was easier than trying to strike up a conversation. Of course, he might understand English a lot better than he spoke it, but I didn't think so. He was watching a weight-lifting competition, I could tell that much, and there was a lot of grunting and groaning and roars of effort and crashes of the great weights coming down under more or less control. I couldn't see any pattern in his reactions and watched only to be polite. I couldn't quite understand his interest. Perhaps he too felt the strangeness of being with someone he couldn't converse with. I had made it pretty clear that he wasn't 'scoring' with me. I was just being friendly – and not that friendly either. It was time to go, before his attention focused on me again, so I finished my beer and gathered up my stuff.

I slid off my stool, and moved behind it to make my goodbye. He pulled his attention away from the screen.

'We go?' he said.

'No,' I said. 'I'm going now.'

'We go,' he said. And now it wasn't a question.

He smiled again. I had trouble with that smile. It was contagious. I smiled back. Big mistake.

'We go . . .' He was stuck for the word. His hands made frustrated gestures. Then he had a breakthrough. 'We go . . .'

and he held up two fingers pointing downwards and made a walking motion with them.

'We go for a walk?' I said.

'Yes!'

He was so pleased that I had understood, his face, his angel's face, was alight. Quickly he slipped off his stool. He obviously took my translation for agreement and I had no way short of out and out rudeness to dissuade him. Somehow I couldn't bring myself to be that rude to that shining face. This is how it starts, I thought, with misunderstandings. And in the morning you're another statistic on a mortuary slab. Are you crazy?

Quickly I tried to think of places to go with him where there would be lots of people. This shouldn't be difficult – the town was bursting with tourists come to watch the Games. He might even be one of them. The tracksuit was a bit of a problem. It was really gruesome – the sort of thing that wives sneak out at night to burn because the husband lives in it. The knees sagged and there were threadbare patches. At least it looked reasonably clean. Leaving aside the large number of places that wouldn't let him in wearing any kind of tracksuit, I cringed thinking what I would do if anyone I knew saw me with him dressed like that. Surely no tourist would stuff something so unpleasant into a suitcase and take it on holiday? It really bugged me, that tracksuit. But if I could only shuck the thought of it from my mind we might have a pleasant walk. I looked down at his feet. He had on a pair of what looked like expensive trainers and no socks. Well, my mother always used to say that if you wanted to know what a person was like you only needed to look at their feet. I determined to concentrate on his feet and not the tracksuit. It was just a pity that you saw a lot more of the tracksuit than you did of the feet.

I looked at my watch: nine o'clock. It was dark out. I needed a well-lit and populated place. With the heat a good option was likely to be the park down the road. It was brightly lit on summer nights. There was a little lake, and a fine fountain which made the air cool and gave a breeze. It was always busy. We could go there.

'Come on then,' I said.

The barman gave me a look. I realised that he thought I was a hooker. Damn. I wouldn't be able to come here again. Next time I want to meet someone for a drink after work it won't be Marianne.

After the air-conditioning in the bar, stepping into the evening air was a nasty shock. It felt like wrapping a warm, wet towel round your face. It made me gasp. He looked concerned. I made a fanning motion with my hand and smiled. He nodded and smiled back. I walked towards the park. He asked no questions. I began to drip. I looked at him. He was dripping too. Not surprising in that jogging suit. Shorts and a vest would have been more sensible.

It was only a block to the corner of the park. You can see the fountain from the gates. I pointed to it as we got near.

'It will be cool there,' I said, slowly and distinctly. 'Nice.'

'Nice,' he repeated and smiled that amazing smile.

In the streetlight the shadows under his eyes were very pronounced. I felt rather sorry for him.

As we walked across the grass I tried something.

'Where do you come from?'

But it was no good. He looked at me, and his hands sketched their frustration again. Then he gave me that universal shrug of not-knowing that is unmistakable and I knew that whatever level we might communicate on it would not be verbal.

The fountain was alluring, but we didn't need to go that far. We were well onto the grassed area when the sprinklers came on. It was a shock, although a pleasant one, and I squealed. He laughed out loud – the first time I had heard him laugh. It was a pleasant, mid-brown sound and I turned to look at him as the water rained onto us. He stripped off his jogging jacket. He was bare-chested underneath. I realised why he had kept the jacket on so long. I gasped. What a body! He wasn't a tall man, nor bulky – I had been able to tell that much, tracksuit or not – but he was perfectly muscled. This was a man who spent serious amounts of time in a gym somewhere. The body of an angel to go with the face. He stood in the rain from the sprinklers with his arms outstretched, looking more angelic by the minute. I would not have been surprised to see wings at his shoulders. Then he began to spin. The wet tracksuit jacket flapped me in the face. The next time it came my way I ducked. The third time he threw it to me and I caught it. Yuk. Then he stopped spinning and held up a finger. Another international gesture, it said 'Watch'. Then he began to turn cartwheels, very good cartwheels such as I had not been able to do even at high school. He cartwheeled fluidly away from me some twenty paces, then cartwheeled back. Others had walked into the sprinklers' spray and he had an audience. One or two people clapped.

He acknowledged his public and held up that finger again. Now he was flick-flacking across the grass and back again. His audience grew and this time the applause was stronger and longer. A crowd was gathering around us. Now he was doing handsprings, on to his hands and up again; now he was walking on his hands, walking upside down around me. The crowd continued to grow and the applause did too as the fake rain fell and soaked us all to the skin.

He bobbed up beside me, right way up again, breathing a little quickly. He made an elegant bow to the crowd and took his jacket back from me. Then he put his hand under my elbow and steered me through the people and away. The sprinklers went off. The crowd gave a sort of moan of disappointment at the end of the show and the end of the shower, and it began to resolve itself into couples and families again.

Couples and families and me, on my own in the park with a stranger. Oddly I had more confidence in him now. Why does one tend to believe in people with talent? There is no reason why only stupid people should be killers and rapists and thieves. Nevertheless I didn't mind his hand underneath my elbow. His touch was hot. I liked it.

We got away from the people – the people I had been at pains to mingle with a little while earlier – and walked down towards the water. He was still breathing quickly from his tumbling. He turned to me and tried again.

'I score very good!'

His hands made rolling motions in the air. This time I could only agree. He scored very good at that alright.

'Yes,' I said.

We were soaked right through. My thin cotton things would soon dry. His jogging pants would take a lot longer. They clung to his legs.

'You're very wet,' I said slowly, pointing to his legs.

He laughed. Oh, it was a pleasant sound.

'Let's walk round the lake,' I said. 'We'll dry off quicker.'

I made the walking gesture with my fingers that he had used before.

'Walk.'

And he made the little walking gesture too. We both laughed this time.

The lake looked very pretty in the lights – lights round it, and lights shining up through the patterns the fountain made.

'Nice,' he said, and pointed to the lights.

I think I taught him a new word. Pity it wasn't a more meaningful one. We've kind of done 'nice' to death. Oh well.

Around the side of the lake there were some concessions selling Coke and pizza and hot dogs and pretzels and stuff. It smelled good. I remembered I had been hungry.

'Do you want to get some pizza?' I asked him.

'Pizza!'

That seemed conclusive, so I joined a queue. We were soon served. I didn't even try to ask him what he wanted, just got two big slices with everything on. We strolled on a ways until we came to the little arena. There's a big curved bank goes up around a flat semicircle with the lake as a backdrop. They have acts there some evenings. With the Games on and the park full you could bet there'd be something on tonight. We sat down and tackled the pizza. It was good. He had trouble with the big droopy triangle of dough. I wondered if he'd ever eaten it before. Difficulty didn't stop him though and he finished it in short order. He caught my eye as I ate my own slice and made another gesture. Thumbs up. Good. I smiled at him.

It wasn't many minutes before something started to happen on the D below us. Half a dozen people in bright costumes that might have been medieval came capering on to the grass. My angel sat up a little straighter. The medieval ones did some tumbling and built towers of themselves, and one of them did fire-eating. My angel was absorbed, mouth slightly open, faint bright smile on his face, greasy with pizza. It wasn't the best show I've seen there, but it was nicely done.

After about half an hour they bowed and skipped off. Now things would get tricky, I thought. With nothing external to engage my friend's attention I'd have to work harder. But I was relaxed about it, the pizza had been good, the night was balmy here, the traffic noise was just a kind of purr in the dark. I was having a good time, I realised – as good as you can have with a companion who doesn't speak a word of your language.

The troupe had barely left the stage and I was still clapping when suddenly he grabbed my wrist. It made me jump, I can tell you. Still I didn't snatch it back straight off. I looked at him, and he was trying to see the time on my watch. His grip was fierce, but I twisted my arm around so that the lights shone on it, to be helpful.

He found what he needed – and he wasn't pleased about it. He dropped my arm and balled his fists and banged them into the grass on either side of him. My arm was still in the air, on its way back to me, so that I could rub it. He'd really hurt me. I didn't get a chance to do it myself because he caught it up again – much gentler this time – and stroked my hand. There was a big red mark coming there. He looked really sorry. Then he kissed the back of my hand, then the front, then he put my hand over his heart. Then he gave it back to me. I was about to try and say something about all this, but I didn't get a chance. As soon as he'd finished his dumbshow he got to his feet, picked up his wet jacket, kissed his fingers to me and set off jogging towards the gate we'd come in by, putting his jacket on as he ran.

So he was Cinderella? Just as things had been getting interesting. Although I was relieved in one way, I was real sorry that he'd taken off like that. When he had kissed my hand I had realised that I really wanted to know what a kiss on the lips would have been like, and after that – well, who knew? And now he was trotting out of my life. In the time it had taken me just to think those few things – well, I had rather dwelled on the kissing part – he'd gone through the park gate into the dark. I looked at my watch, in case it told me what had spooked him. Ten thirty – make what you can of that, I thought.

I didn't sit there long after that. I picked myself up and got a bus, which joined an endless jam of traffic which all seemed to want to go my way. It took me an hour to get home. I showered and went straight to bed. It's funny how tiring sitting still in the heat can be.

I slept hard and woke late. I had to scurry to catch the bus in. Same thing, stop-go all the way. I finished my magazine and was reduced to looking out of the window at the jam and reading the back of the newspaper nearest me. This was the pits – the back pages are always sport and I don't like sport. It makes me feel more tired to read about sport than it does to sit in the heat and sweat. Still, what can you do?

But not today; today just reading that paper made me sweat – because it was him. It was a crappy picture but it was him alright: the pale hair and eyes, the dark rings around the eyes accentuated by the heavy contrast in the photograph, the beautiful smile almost ethereal. I strained to read the caption. If we hadn't stopped for a gridlock, giving me a good long look at it, I'd have snatched that paper right out of the hands of the man who was reading it. The caption said: 'Aleksandr Vorodovich from Russia, who took the gold medal in the individual men's gymnastics competition yesterday.'

I thought of 'You score no' and my clenched fist. Then the rest of that evening came back to haunt me. He had won a gold medal and all I could do for him was teach him one more English word and feed him pizza. He seemed OK with that – so why did I feel such a jerk?

7

South | R.D. Malagola

Ray and Rita Tabarnac sat up high in the cab of the silver, bullet-shaped camper van and eased on to the south road, out of town. They moved slowly, patiently, with weight. With hundreds of rehearsal miles behind them, on wide and narrow roads alike, up hill and down, with easy pacing on the freeways and fist-tight manoeuvres in city sidestreets, they were ready for the real thing. No question about it, this load was on the heavy side for a lifelong Pinto man, but a thing of beauty nevertheless: the tube trailer hitched on behind, and the 35-foot cabin cruiser sitting pretty in its cradle. This was the future.

No more selling hardware for him, after twenty-five years of hardselling hardware, no more TV sport and DIY and unprofound consequences. No more hardware for her, no more housekeeping and active mothering, after a lifetime. Camper-keeping and boatkeeping from now on. With her son, Charlie, dead and buried in Kansas City, mothering had become a solitary affair, and only indulged during the few unsullied moments she managed to pluck from the many mundane.

White mist hung on burdened trees, tugged and billowed out

at them as they swept past. Cool, early-morning air whipped in, lashed pink grins on to their faces and tin whistles to their ears. Ray laid his hand on Rita's as they rolled along an empty highway.

They'd left no trace behind, not a thing that might reclaim them: no store, no house, no bank accounts, no trunks of memories, no friendships they couldn't live without. It was all here, in the hardly used camper, bought cheaply from Rita's cousin, Jerry, down in Quebec. In the old boat too, which Ray had spent six summers restoring: green and red now, with shining brass and darkly lacquered wood, she was as sweet on the eye as she was strong. They called her the *Cherie*, after Ray's grandmother.

'And plenty of space for hitch-hikers,' Ray observed, with a hint of pride.

'If we so desire,' Rita corrected.

'I didn't mean . . .'

'Of course you didn't, honey.' She closed her eyes, and Ray kept his on the road.

In Moose Jaw, to the south, Ray and Rita pulled in through thin forest and made camp beside a lake, and here listened in to a lofty wind, scudding soft, vanilla-cream clouds across the treetops, to frogs arising and rooks settling. A couple of times, Ray caught himself feeling for the remote control, thinking he might flip to ice hockey on another channel. Here, to the south of Moose Jaw, their untroubled dreams were accompanied by the sound of monster fish jumping into the night. Like shy Olympians, these leapers crossed, twisted, jackknifed, and dropped cleanly back into the black water; just small splashes, just echoes, the sounds of one lip smacking, and no applause. Ray, an urban man in all but his heart, felt no fear here, true enough. The fear of going back was the only one he carried. Rita, between the sheets, slept like the nearly dead; without memory or desire, without dread.

In Pierre, to the south-east, they joined up with a bunch of young weekenders: all up here to keep from suicide, it seemed. There, in a high-timber clearing, a haphazard clutch of teepees, one-man tents, blanket bivouacs and bedrolls. An arc of Harleys, rusting pickups and VWs, and a tangle of mountain bikes. No children to be seen. Bonfires, great and small, sent conversations into a swift sky, as the twang and cackle of guitars and harmonicas lazily chased after the smoke. Talk was cheap, interlaced with coughing and laughter. Ray and Rita sat right in at the heart, swigging on the Jim Beam, pulling on the sweetweed that curled their way from time to time. Oddly, most of the talk up here was about down there, about homes and cities, about dirt and grind, and escape. They spoke about 'reality' and hallucination (more coughing than laughing now), and about lost and found.

Jack, a mechanic from Huron, reminded Rita of Charlie: something small in the way he held his head when he gazed into space and kept his mouth shut. When he spoke and winced, he reminded her of a mechanic. And in the night, she dreamed undead, of dark hands ingrained with grease, with nails chewed down, with callouses sliding roughly on her thighs, bunching and crushing the blue cotton of a dress she'd once owned. She cried out weakly as they pushed and snagged, and carried with them the stench of whisky, dope and lust; the stench of Charlie.

Somewhere between Lexington and Red Cloud, they picked up an oldtimer by the name of Coop, a boxcar hobo of the old school, with authentic parasites that jitterbugged and jived at all hours, and a deadly wine-stained breath which never slept. His crumpled eyes were clean though; beady like a buzzard's, and watchfully disinterested. He was eighty-three years old.

'You lost something?' he asked, paused, 'or just plain lost?' The timing was good, and a hint of a joke.

'Not lost,' Rita replied.

'If you say so.' And that was the end of that. Somewhere in the middle of nowhere, in the middle of the day, he asked to be put down, and trudged off without a word, headed true south.

In Kansas City they visited Charlie's grave. They stood quietly there for several minutes, listened to a whippy little wind as it capered through long grass and short memories, took a wry satisfaction in the laughably neat, white picket fences and crew-cut lawns of their son's final resting place. Twenty years of hard, bright-burning life didn't get a mention here. 'What a mess,' Rita sighed. Ray shot her a sideways look, tried to read where she was coming from. He said nothing.

Once back in the camper, and out of the blue, Ray and Rita became stricken by an inflammation, a time-blunted sadness, found themselves suddenly and painfully entangled with seatbelts, cassettes, route maps and Thermoses, in a twisted version of what Ray called 'Grand Missionary'. Now his naked buttocks flared and flattened as they pumped against the cold glass of the windscreen, and Rita kept her eyes bright open, stared out across a wasteland of dusted headstones; and the prairie beyond, she assumed.

As they played canasta amid the debris, all that remained memorable, by its labour and bruises, was the undressing. The rest had returned to the blue.

In Abilene Rita and Ray danced a waltz. It was easily remembered, like riding a bicycle.

In Pecos they talked about Geronimo and the Grateful Dead, and not for the first time. They ate chilli dogs and tacos and drank Budweisers. Here too they made love, up in the boat's cabin, high and swaying on top of its trailer. Sweeter and sweeter, mile by mile.

In Chihuahua they talked about God.

In Durango, to the north, up in the thin air, Ray talked *to* God, or so it seemed. He was not aware of any hallucinogens imbibed along the way, but knew that refreshment accepted casually on these high roads had to be taken with a degree of faith. And yet, when he looked around him, all else was as it should be, in place and harmonious. The wind was raw and the sky blue, and no birds sang or chaffed; it was just the rock that didn't sit right.

'Sure thing, a Nappa Valley red, but nothing special' is what Rita heard. She looked up and, before she could respond, realised that her husband, as far as she could make out, was talking wines with a couch-sized boulder; close up and animated, Ray, with a furrowed brow, now contemplated how, exactly, a boulder took its wine, the mechanics of something like that.

As the sun descended on to a distant, jagged horizon, turned to rust, Ray uncorked a second bottle. Between visits to the rock, bottle in hand, and modest pourings here and there, he assumed a good-looking, cross-legged position nearby, and discussed with the deity (as he later explained to Rita) any number of things, from real estate to Perkins engines, from *déjà vu* to decals. Rita was content to listen in to her husband's stuttering monologue, to man the first-aid kit, to haunt the peripherals, and to make no judgements. He was beginning to sound a little drunk.

Rita heard it like this: '*Oh yes, that's the plan. We'll transfer to the boat somewhere along the Chile coast, wherever the water looks good, you know . . .*'

And like this: '*You think so? Well, we hadn't thought of that, I must say . . .*'

And so on, like this: '*Why not! Because I'm not completely nuts, that's why not!*'

This: '*Oh really, and go where, exactly?*'

And this: '*South! South of Cape Horn! Are you kidding?*'

What's this? '*Of course you do. I've heard you . . .*'

And: '*OK. But South of Cape Horn . . .*'

Ray appeared to think about it, stole a look at Rita. She was smiling but not laughing, and weary now; there would be more. From her bed, Ray's voice turned into bubbling water, into trouted streams.

In the dead of night, Rita heard her husband crawling into the camper, into bed. He was breathing heavily, and seemed to be already naked. When they awoke the next morning, somewhat later than usual, the boulder was gone. They talked about it.

In San José, in the city itself, as a dusty evening took hold, Rita

and Ray saw three shadowy men beating another in a rubbish-
strewn alley. And Ray surprised himself, did what he'd always
hoped he would do, what he had, many times, dreamt of doing
in his snug, unheroic bed: he leapt from the camper, howling like
a wolf, like a banshee, surged perfectly towards certain death.
He was fearless, crazy. The three men, momentarily confused,
tricked by such perfection, and caught in twilight, did not wait for
the unknown; they fled separately down well-known boltholes,
slid into a yellow night. Rita now cradled the broken and dead
body of a twelve-year-old boy, stroked his shiny, blood-soaked
hair until the police and ambulance arrived. No people came to
watch, and those that passed by kept moving.

In Iquique they parked up on an endless beach from which the
Earth's curve was seen to be no joking matter. Some bikers with
bedrolls and big music, a retired couple from Baton Rouge, an
Italian writer, and a TV crew from England making a travel
show. And not much else.

Anton, the travel-show presenter, planned a brief and pawky
exchange with any one of them who would stand still long
enough. 'D'you come here often? Ha ha!'; anyway, these things
always came together in the cutting-room. Bruno, the writer,
wasn't actually writing at present. He was, he claimed, recovering
from too much writing. 'I just jumped in my pickup one morning,
back in São Paulo, and kept driving,' he told them. 'See, I feel
good now, almost ready,' he explained. And what did he write?
'I came for *Magic Realism*, obviously, but that turned out to be
shit.' He sighed. 'Now I do Universal . . . and drink heavily.'

'And this boat of yours, Ray, what's the story with the boat?'

If there was a story here, Anton felt sure that this was the way to go.

'It means we can carry on . . . when the land runs out.'

'Land runs out? How d'you mean, exactly? What land?'

'Down on the Cape.'

'Pardon me? . . . Not Cape Horn?'

'Sure.'

'Ah huh, and you're going where, exactly?'

'South.'

'South. South of Cape Horn? . . . Ah huh . . . interesting.'

'We hope so.'

'But in that pissy little thing? You can't be serious?'

'Forever south. Why not?' Ray was beginning to lose what little interest he'd started this with.

'"Forever south." It's a wind-up, right?'

'It's just a concept,' Rita intervened, a little tetchy, 'an idea: forever south. You know.'

'Right.' Anton didn't know; he didn't like this story any more, just didn't get it. 'Right, an idea. I can see that. But it's an idea that gets you both killed, isn't it?' And he was beginning to like the sound of that.

'Don't they all?' Rita betrayed her fatigue.

'Great. OK, that'll do it, people. Let's move on.' Anton moved on, on down the beach towards biker cool and some homely Baton Rouge wisdom; something quirky, something for TV, at least.

Bruno got to his feet, unwound the Italian flag he was wearing around his waist, stood before them naked, and closed his eyes.

'You're sure you need the boat?' he asked. He didn't wait for a reply, simply loped off towards the ocean, and, once there, plunged unflinchingly into the shallow waters.

In Tocopilla, before and after, Rita skipped through the last chapters of *Le Grand Meaulnes*, which she knew like the back of her hand, and began reading *The Man Who Loved Children*, which she didn't. Ray was in the middle of both *Bill the Galactic Hero* and *Auto-da-Fé*; he tried to maintain a balance whenever possible. A bit of a literary funambulist, he liked to think himself, with striped umbrella in one hand and garish paperbacks in the other.

In Antofagasta, Ray finished *Bill the Galactic Hero* with a chuckle, and gave up on the Canetti, wrist-whipping it, like a clumsy Frisbee, into a speeding ditch. He started reading road signs instead.

In Taltal, they talked.

'You feel good, Rita?' Ray asked, without meaning anything by it.

'Does it matter?' Rita threw it away.

'It does to me.'

'Good.'

'All miracles aside, I mean.'

'Ah . . . talking boulders, and the like. "Forever south."'

'Sure, and Italian writers and dead boys. And all the things we *didn't* see.'

'They don't matter any more.'

'No. But we *knew*, didn't we?'

'We wanted to know.'

'And we still do, right?'

'Turn round, go back, re-enlist, is that what you're saying?'

'That's what I'm saying, but not to screw you up. Just for clarity.'

'No need.'

'No.'

Then, and truthfully: 'I still want things, Ray, don't imagine I don't. I want to laugh.'

'Of course. We'll do that. And absorb; we do all that now.'

'Not just you.'

'No.'

Then: 'Bruno made a pass at me, you know.'

'That must have been funny.'

'In a way.'

'Just kidding, honey. I couldn't blame him.'

'Better than a cold rock, anyway.'

'Sure thing.'

'*Was* it female?'

'How the hell would I know?'

'You looked flushed. That look of yours.'

'I was drunk.'

'He was Italian, of course. He called me *"Bella"*.'

In Valparaiso, they filled the 'space for hitch-hikers'; with Juanita and Annie from LA. 'Honeymooners', who had abandoned their fatally wounded Datsun Cherry in Quintero, and now continued, on the thumb, towards Concepción, and interesting trains home. For Rita, this ride was affecting but not something she could explain; everything that selling hardware had never been. For Ray, it was another stretch of road.

Annie and Juanita were in love, of course, but not to the detriment of the host-and-guest relationship. They caressed carelessly, in passing, and disengaged at the drop of a hat; over the years they had disengaged at the drop of many hats: hard hats, ski hats, sombreros, panamas and, of course, red-necked Stetsons aplenty. They were old hands at that.

'Sure,' Annie acceded, 'but that's like *south*-of-south, utterly south. No other directions but. And just a touch crazy, am I right?'

'Honey, they're talking symbols,' Juanita admonished. 'It's not like they're going to tip over the edge of the world. I think it's cool.'

'Yeah, sure, I know that. But, Jesus, it's so utterly . . . so utterly . . . utter.' She wasn't happy with that, of course. She grimaced.

'It doesn't mean anything. It's bare bones,' Rita explained, or imagined she did, 'pared down.'

'Pared down? Pared as in cut, right?'

'Chainsawed!' Ray was talking hardware suddenly, and with a small whoop. Then, in a steadier tone, 'With all the crap cut away, I mean.'

'Just like all this,' Rita added.

'All this?'

'All the lost and found.' Rita *was* emphatic, but didn't yet know how to sound it.

In Concepción, Juanita and Annie set off, hand in hand towards the railway station, heading north, small knapsacks bouncing on small backsides, baseball caps askance. Ray put some Doors on the CD as they rolled majestically through an early-morning traffic of lunatics.

In Osorno, they ate inch-thick beef rump, stewed in the last of the Nappa Valley wine. Afterwards they lay naked and unquilted on the bed, and sipped rum. They played there with each other for several hours. Toyed and teased and trifled, without making love. And then they slept. In the middle of the night, they awoke simultaneously, only to find themselves coupled hard together; and not in the Grand Missionary this time. Rita laughed suddenly and made him squeal.

In Cochrane, up and east, Ray played 'Three Steps to Heaven' as they entwined. Rita gasped in the thin air.

In Puerto Natales, down the road there, they wore Canadian clothes against the bleating wind and tarmac skies. Here they made love for warmth.

In Punta Arenas, they booked into a hotel close to the water, which wasn't cheap, and looked at the truth, which was. Here, they came to understand at last that nothing was true, that nothing had happened . . . How could it have? No lake in Moose Jaw, no grave in Kansas City, no speaking rock, no back-alley blood; those places belonged to others. No endless beaches and oceans, no Italian writer with flirtation on his mind, no LA lovers, and no Pan-American Highway, heading forever south.

With a new incredulity and an old faith, they launched the *Cherie* into harboured calm, and anchored her there; she shipped no water. They sold their $25,000 camper for $1,000, bought goods, provisions and fuel, and skiffed them across. On a morning as gentle as a lullaby, they set sail on a southerly course.

Ray navigated these complex waterways with the help of state-of-the-art equipment, local advice, and the stars themselves. Now, in the absence of road signs, he took to studying charts and maps and celestial guides. He chain-ate gingernuts and chocolate-chip cookies as he read, and drank Italian coffee. Rita mostly read, or cooked squid in batter, or sat out on deck and watched the stars for reasons which owed nothing to navigation. Charlie slept in the stern, curled into himself, in his sleeping bag, much like any untroubled four year old. His parents took turns around the deck, turns in which they passed him by, kept a weather eye on him.

The seas, now open and uncluttered with land, remained freakishly calm; more Mediterranean than south-of-south. The sun lolled lifelessly, as did the moon in its shift, both hanging in a hefty, unbreezed air, like inflamed tongues. Ray and Rita spoke little now; they too curled into themselves. They expected a storm. Sometimes they allowed the boat to drift, with engine dead, directionless and patient, and then rectified to a southerly course. Other ships were seen, great and distant hulks with imagined rust and ghostly creakings, and no souls to interfere with their programmed progress. From the *Cherie*, these monsters were too exotic to threaten, indifferent to that which could not hinder them or cause anything more dangerous than a small bump in their night; that which was not edible.

As time passed, Rita and Ray improvised: they learnt to rumba and mambo, listened to the Ramones, played backgammon and Bolivia, caught herring and bottled them for rollmops, experimented with Prozac and Mandrax, sketched one another, videoed the slow-swelling water; and took their strolls around the deck. They no longer knew what day it was.

'Do you know something, Raymond, you dance quite beautifully,' said Rita, out of a far blue.

'Really?'

'Such a shame we've done so little. So much time spent *not* dancing.'

'Watching TV.'

'Washing and wishing.'

'We could try a tango next. I've got a book.'

'Why not.'

When there's no frame in which to fit time, there is no picture, no dots to be joined up, no pixel. So Ray and Rita began to tango in the early hours of the morning; no more precise than that. They slept as the sun climbed, ate breakfast for tea, lunched at midnight, danced until dusk, and worshipped the sun in its absence. Once, around a sun-up or sundown (crepuscular, at least), they saw a blemish on the distant south-east waters. Or did they? Whipped cream and mango?

After the tango, they did salsa, samba and cha-cha-cha. After Grand Missionary, they did doggie, Java, vulgar and mitre; they even attempted the impossible. They did Proust out loud, and Pynchon under their breath, Colette when they couldn't sleep, and Joyce when they could; they even did Bentham, for the jokes;

and beginners' yoga too, en passant. And they watched forward, over a gently lifting bow, as a slow, dark blanket of cloudside reared up and then seeped into a pool-blue sky. It was true, like bruised fruit. In the night (or day), in their bunk, they felt an unhurried, fairy wind licking and whispering about them. On deck, in the daylight, the sky had divided into two equal halves overhead: pale and cloudless astern, bleak and stonewall for'ard. They began to pitch and roll, but only lightly still; enough to find sea legs with. A damp fret laced across their faces and bare arms, like kisses. And now a sound, a slow-rolling thunder, a deep and vast memory of lost and found, which held them there and purloined any notions of hard-won wisdom from the years.

At last they pulled away, went below, finding everything above to be hopelessly true. They checked around, tidied a little, took peeks astern, for Charlie in his bag, astern where the sky to be seen remained entirely blue. They held each other's hands, they danced to Charley Musselwhite's 'Christo Redemptor', like the old days, like teenagers. They dreamed of riding rogue elephants, switchbacks, Calgary broncos; they did dream. Of artillery hits in the Crimea, heat-seekers in the desert, the Grateful Dead, *live*! True dreams and genetic memories.

In time, or in a moment of it, they rose up, Rita and Ray, into the last breath of the world. It was a roar. Now the world was full of water; not rain, but water. Water as crystal, as the air itself, as the first roaring breath of the world. No pitching, no rolling, a dead calm below. A smooth glide, unpowered and powerless, towards the brink.

There ahead, as they held each other gently at waist and shoulder, the end of the world slid ever closer. No sea, no land, no form, and stretching away, if not for ever, then for a very long way indeed. Neither light nor dark; not truly. Not warm or cold, not real or unreal. It came upon them like a born-again sloth. Ray and Rita, with redundant sea legs under them, sturdy on the *Cherie*'s deck, pushed out into the empty, hung there like a sun, like a red giant, like Nijinsky. No breath, and no sound now.

'Not many supertankers in these parts, I guess,' Ray quipped. Rita smiled at him.

And now they fell, without a falling. Was that White Light or a star so close? It all turned, inverted, cascaded, shone, took them away. Charlie joined them there, in his scarlet pyjamas. He yawned and tried to take in the view.

'There, there, sleepyhead.' Ray squeezed his boy's shoulder. 'It's just fine.'

'It is now,' Rita agreed, as she kissed Charlie's cheek and took his hand; 'and much as I expected.'

The Rembrandt Sisters | Adèle Geras

Rivka, my younger daughter, has wrapped me in a lacy blue shawl for the Sabbath. In spite of the heat I'm swaddled like a baby. Death is perceived as cold, even in these temperatures. I am near death and so I must be feeling chilly: this is how Rivka reasons. I haven't the strength to speak and, to tell the truth, I don't really mind. Perhaps Death is a source of cold after all, and I am standing nearer to him than I think.

Rivka has left her tapestry at the foot of the bed and gone to do the things she left undone last night, the little things she always forgets to do before the Sabbath arrives. I can hear her now, tearing pieces of lavatory paper off the roll . . . so many pieces. Well, they're all coming today. Every scrap will be needed. All those glasses of lemon tea and milky coffee. Niagara. That's the name written on the inside of the lavatory bowl, and Niagara will be foaming and frothing today. One tug of the metal chain and the roaring will start. Rivka has put the paper on the lavatory window sill, and when she comes back she'll pick up the tapestry. They all think that just because I'm dying I don't know what goes on here during the Sabbath. This one stitches, that one smokes, someone uses the telephone. They run to the Mayovskys' flat. They go and take forbidden puffs from cigarettes up there on the roof. At the Mayovskys' they eat abominations. Filth. I can smell it from here, the steak fried in butter. A person can weep.

Dying will be a relief in many ways. I can see too much, hear too much, and I've lived so long that I know almost everything that's going on. The silence of death will be a blessing. My head is crowded with too many people. Not only my children and their children, my friends and my neighbours, but also an assortment of phantoms, misty shadows of the dead who drift into the corners of my bedroom like leaves tumbled by the wind. My mother, blessed be her memory, has placed herself on the linen chest and will not move. My poor husband whispers in my ear during the night and I blush just to remember the things he speaks of . . . and my poor little dead babies. They were so small and new when they left me that they didn't even leave ghosts behind them. That's how insubstantial they were. Tiny lives, tiny little lives, like curls of smoke. There is never silence any more. My ears ring with dozens of conversations that fade and swell and fade again, like the voices on the radio that blossom and then die.

From far away across the city, I can hear my elder son Isaac quarrelling with Rachel, his wife. He's putting his shoes on, ready to walk across Jerusalem to this flat. Rachel is tying a scarf around her hair, for my sake.

She says: 'When was the last time you came with me to my father's house on the Sabbath? Every week we have to trudge for miles in this heat, so hot that a person can melt.'

'It's not so often, once a week,' Isaac answers mildly. 'And my mother is dying.'

I am not the only reason he comes, of course. There is also Pnina Hausman. She and her sister Shoshanna live over there, in one of the flats opposite. The Hausman Girls, we call them. They're at least fifty, the Girls. They are dressing for the Sabbath. Soon they will come and visit me. It is the highlight of their week. Oh, I can see them. Pnina is ready. Look what a sober little dress she is wearing! Her hair is still lovely. She is tying it up in a knot, so that no one will guess how beautiful it is. Pnina uses her clothes to hide in. Shoshanna is still in her petticoat of pink silk. Old and darned, but such a colour, like a baby's cheek. And silk, of course. Shoshanna likes pretty things. She wants not to grow old.

She says: 'Do you remember the Rembrandt Sisters? That wasn't their name, of course, only their berets . . . Rembrandt berets we called them. They looked so strange, like two brown velvet pancakes sliding down over their faces . . . d'you remember?'

Pnina answers: 'They've been dead for years.'

'But,' says Shoshanna, 'we used to see them out of this window and you used to say . . . it was always you and I only agreed with you . . . we'll never be like that, Shoshanna, you said. Never. How terrible to walk in the sun at that age arm in arm with your *sister*!'

'Come away from that window, Shoshanna. Everyone will see you.'

'And so? These breasts like ripe melons, this skin like velvet.

All right, a slightly over-ripe melon, and velvet that's lost a little of its bloom, perhaps, but still. I think the neighbours will enjoy it. Genzel will lift his head from the inside of the pickle barrel and realise that there is more to life than his wife's drawers. I've seen them, Pnina. They look like flour sacks, hanging up to dry. Poor old Genzel!'

The Hausman Girls . . . there they are, getting ready. They come here every Saturday. They say it's to see me, and to talk to their friend Rivka, my daughter, who, because she has no husband but a dead war hero instead, is free to talk to them and free to put shawls around me as though I were her child. Really, really, Pnina is still in love with my Isaac. I came upon them once, more than thirty years ago, up on the roof, kissing. Who knows how matters would have turned out if I'd been later by a few minutes? Perhaps he would never have married Rachel. I don't like Rachel, but I keep my mouth shut, naturally. Oh, she's religious and an excellent mother and her gefilte fish is the best in Jerusalem, but I can't like her. Her mouth is forever clicking and clacking, and if she opens her legs once every three months, my son can count himself fortunate. It's a blessing that he's happy in his work. All over the city, one brick on another, he's putting up walls of butter-yellow stone.

Isaac and Rachel have arrived. They have kissed me and sat beside my bed and now they've gone. Rivka is giving them kugel and glasses of amber-coloured tea. I'm pretending to be asleep. When he was a little boy, Isaac used to be terrified of the Rembrandt Sisters. Chaim, my other son, had told him that they were witches, with faces wrinkled like old paper. They had tin tubs, Chaim said, just like the ones used for the washing, and into these tubs they put chopped-up pieces of the children they'd managed to get hold of. Chaim . . . he was the one with the imagination. Perhaps he should have had another kind of life. What can he do with an imagination, selling basins and lavatory bowls all day long from that small shop? Dvora, his wife, looks pinched and sour like a lemon. The whole town knows that Chaim has other women. Dvora knows too but she loves him. Rivka, Naomi my other daughter, even Rachel, everyone tells Dvora over and over again to leave him, divorce him, find another man, but she shakes her head and says nothing. She loves him. Also, what would she live on?

Naomi and her husband David have come. Naomi is tidying my cupboard. She tidies everything. She arranges everything. When they were girls, she and Rivka liked the Rembrandt Sisters. Naomi admired their straight backs, and the fact that they never took off those berets, even in the hottest weather. Also, as Rivka pointed out, they looked as though they knew where they were going.

'Rivka,' Naomi says now, 'how do you have the patience for all those tiny stitches? All those different colours . . . and how don't you go crazy without a pattern to follow? There's nothing printed on the canvas. Nothing to tell you what to do next.'

'It's like life,' says Rivka and Naomi laughs.

'A philosopher, suddenly.'

'Really,' Rivka smiles. 'Just like life. You never know what will happen next, or what colour it'll be. Days and days go by with everything flat and yellow, and then all at once I reach for a blue thread – clear, pale, shining blue – and there's the sky after that desert of yellow. It's a kind of excitement, seeing what comes next, how one colour edges into another.'

I know more about that tapestry than she does. She started it two years ago, in 1956 when Moshe was killed. It's still not finished. She started it in order to fill her head with colours and empty it of any object that she could put a name to. In her canvas there were no guns, tanks, bombs, shells, no metal and no fire. But I see the long lines of red spreading out and criss-crossing the yellow, like veins threading through the sand.

Naomi, Rivka and David drift away. Chaim and Dvora come and kiss me and drift away after them. Some of my children 'go and say hello to the Mayovskys', which is another way of saying they go and make a phone call or smoke a cigarette. Chaim is at this very moment whispering love-words into the black hole of the telephone, and they slide through the wires and into the ear of whichever damp and satiny creature he has torn himself away from . . . oh, I hear him, I hear him!

Rachel and Shoshanna, Rivka and Naomi are in the kitchen preparing the lunch. David and Dvora are with Chaim at the Mayovskys'. Isaac and Pnina are up on the roof, where they spent so much time as children. Everyone is busy. Niagara is silent. The heat is like a shawl over the house, wrapping it up. They all think I'm sleeping.

Pnina comes in and kisses me.

'I'm not feeling too well, Auntie Sarah,' she says. She calls me Auntie Sarah as though she were still a little girl.

'It's the heat,' she goes on. 'I'm going home to lie down.'

She goes, and after lunch Isaac goes to her. They, all of them, think he has walked down the hill to pay a visit to some old friend of his from school, who lives in the house with the rabbit hutch in the garden, round the corner from the hospital; but I know better. I can tell. I saw them. I saw everything happening behind the shutters. There was trembling and sighing and kissing, and her breasts were like ripe pomegranates and his thighs were like fine silver and she allowed him to kiss her with the kisses of his mouth for his love was better than wine. It's all in the Song of Songs: raisins and honey and wine and lilies and roses and pomegranates. Why do I have to describe it?

My last surviving friend, Simha, comes to sit beside my bed after lunch, while the yellow afternoon rubs against the windows. And, oh my goodness, she used to tell some stories about the Rembrandt Sisters!

'They were loose women,' she said to me, long ago. 'Not only half the British army, but also . . . well, you'd never guess to see them walking so demurely down the street in those hats. They used to come and play bridge with my sister. They used to eat her sesame-seed biscuits and crystallised fruit and lick their fingers daintily after each bite . . . and later we found that the eating of my sister's sweets wasn't all that Louisa was doing.' Simha lowered her voice at this point. 'Whenever it was her turn to be dummy, she would disappear and come back later with pink cheeks . . . oh, very pink cheeks and shining eyes and panting a little. You could see her breasts still vibrating under her blouse. Louisa did not believe in brassières. Quivering and wobbling and bobbing about under her blouse they were, like small round animals.'

Simha now sits beside me through the afternoon, clutching on her lap a huge black handbag. In it are her jewels, and there are plenty of them. They are individually wrapped in torn scraps of newspaper. This is what she thinks: anyone looking into my bag will say, 'Ach, it's only a crazy old woman with a bag stuffed full of newspapers,' then they'll leave me alone.

Simha goes home, and Chaim comes to talk to me. He whispers in my ear about Isaac and Pnina. All the time I have been sitting with Simha, dramas have been going on somewhere else . . . on the balcony, on the roof. Even in the bathroom, because I have heard, somewhere in the background, the running and running of water to unredden red eyes, to ease features swollen with tears. Isaac has asked Rachel for a divorce. He loves Pnina, he says. If I had not come up and found them kissing all those years ago, he would have married her, he says. They grew up together, had things in common . . . oh, all this tires me so, and Chaim talks and talks.

'Isaac is an innocent,' he says. 'More innocent than a child who thinks that love is everything. It's a lot, yes, but not everything, because habit is something too, and change is something, and children are something, and disruption of one's life is something, and age is something and, more than all of these, money is a very big something, and so . . . I think Rachel will scream and shout and use delaying tactics . . . and meanwhile Isaac will have grown more accustomed to Pnina's rather middle-aged flesh, and the golden glaze over everything will start to chip away, a little bit more every time they are together.'

My son is a cynic. It's no wonder he's not a believer in love, living day in, day out among the pink porcelain and blue porcelain of bathroom fixtures heaped all around him in the shop.

Evening. Three stars have appeared and the Sabbath is over. Rivka and Naomi will now wash the dishes from the whole of the day's eating, and they'll dry them with whichever towel comes to hand because they think I am beyond knowing or caring. The red-striped towel for meat, and the blue-striped one for milk . . . where's the difference? they would say. Maybe they're right and I shouldn't mind, but I do. There are other senses than sight – smell, for example. Blood. I can smell it on the red-striped towel, deep down, woven into the fabric, and the slightly sour smell of milk in the blue threads. Never mind.

The Hausman Girls are taking off their Sabbath finery. According to Chaim, all their worst fears will be realised and yes, yes, they *will* walk down the street arm in arm like the Rembrandt Sisters. Pnina tells Shoshanna what has happened with Isaac.

She says: 'He loves me. He says he loves me. He says he'll divorce Rachel and marry me.'

'Don't you believe him?'

'When I see the canopy over my head and hear the glass being crushed under his heel, that's when I'll believe. Till then, I will simply live.'

*   *   *

Adèle Geras

There are certain things that will have to be done when I die. Rivka will phone Isaac, Chaim and Naomi. She will phone the doctor and the rabbi, put a notice in the newspaper and weep and weep and sit for seven days, and she will put another colour into the tapestry. She will sew into it a line of tiny black stitches like tears, a thin line that will cross the yellow for deserts and blue for skies, and slice across the long red streams of blood. It will be the making of her tapestry, the finishing touch. Black. A pleasing contrast.

Inside Story | Amy Prior

My father always said that when I was naughty I made Florence Nightingale angry. Of course at that time I never knew who Florence really was. She was just the lady on the ten-pound note who had a furrowed brow and tight lips. The first time it happened was when I poured too much foaming bath oil in the Jacuzzi and the daily had to scrub twice as hard to remove the greasy film that remained. 'You should know by now, Lisa-Lou. No oils in the tub,' Daddy said when he got home from work, and then he reached into his pocket and produced a crumpled ten-pound note. 'You see this, Lisa-Lou,' he said, flattening the paper between the palms of his hands, 'this is Florence Nightingale,' he said, pointing to her face on the note. 'And when you are naughty, you make her angry. See her furrowed brow?' he said.

And after that whenever I was naughty I would look at Florence and she would look at me with those steely eyes of hers and I would think, I have to be a good girl because Florence is watching me. Funny thing is, when I was good I would look at Florence's face and it would have none of the harshness it had when I was naughty. Her eyes sparkled, the corners of her lips upturned slightly. She radiated warmth.

In those days we lived in a mansion along a wide road that led into the centre of Southampton. It was quite a busy road, but we couldn't hear any of the traffic because there was triple glazing at the front of the house. We'd got a pretty hefty relocation fee, my dad said, that's why we could afford to live there. At that time we were moving every few years or so. My dad is a travelling salesman and he moved to wherever business was best. By the time I was thirteen years old I'd lived in Huddersfield, Sutton, Wigan, Birmingham and Crawley.

The things that Daddy said to tempt me to Southampton. He said that in our bathroom there would be solid-gold taps inlaid with semi-precious stones: red ruby for the hot and onyx for the cold. He said that we would have a separate room for each meal we ate. The breakfast room would be sunny in the mornings and always decorated with fresh flowers. The lunch room would be joined to the kitchen by a hatch and would have access to a conservatory in which you could sit admiring orchids. The supper room was to be the grandest room of all. The walls would be covered with a wine-red paper laced with velour ferns. All the furniture was to be coloured dark oak, and we would eat with solid-silver cutlery, the kind the Queen uses.

We had all of these things in Southampton and more.

Daddy got ideas for the house from Uncle Phillip, his only brother, who lived in a show home in Denver, Colorado. He'd moved out there in the late Seventies, before I was born. All we knew about his life was contained in the word-processed letter he wrote to us every Christmas, Mum said he probably sent the same one to everyone he knew back in England. Still, Dad didn't care. 'He's family,' Daddy always said, after reading out what he had to tell us that year, 'and he's done well for himself.'

So when the possibility of the trip came up, all I could think about was seeing the uncle and aunt and cousins I had never met. 'Don't hold out your hopes,' Daddy said for weeks beforehand, 'we might not pull it off.' But at night I would re-read those letters and dream of sharing their luxurious lifestyle. I imagined choosing which of the five bathrooms to use and eating food prepared by their cook. By day we would be stars in *Dynasty*; by night we would be the Waltons. Everyone in my family would say goodnight to one another in turn, and then we would all sleep soundly in our beds until morning.

The reason for the trip was that Daddy's company wanted to expand into the States. His business was films. You know the one where the woman gets poisoned by a creature from Mars and turns into a half-woman, half-alien and her husband only realises when he sees her in the bath? That's one of Daddy's. The plan was Daddy and I were to travel to several American cities, one of them Denver, so he could visit some film distributors to sell them his new films. Mum was going to a health farm to have her insides cleaned out ('I've got to freshen up for the summer,' she always said in early spring), so it was just Dad and me.

Once the trip got the red light from the execs, I busied myself with the practicalities. I bought a brand-new sponge bag with my allowance and filled it with travel toiletries. I also made sure I had clothes for every conceivable change of weather, because

Daddy had told me that the climate was going to be very different in all the cities we visited. But when he saw my bag, he said: 'Anyone would think we were going for two months not two weeks, Lisa-Lou. Cut it down. We can't be carrying all that.'

Before we left, Mum called me up to her dressing-room. I remember she was sitting in front of the mirror, applying eyeliner with a fine brush from a tiny bottle. When she saw my reflection beside her, she patted the corner of her chair and told me to sit down.

'You know, Lisa-Lou,' she said, 'this trip means a lot to your father. They're big deals he's going for. And you've got to help him. Be a lady and wear those suits we picked out for you and you'll make a good impression on all those business people.'

Then she turned to look at me, examining my face as though she had not seen it for a while. 'You know, you've got such beautiful skin,' she said, moving her fingers over my cheek. 'You could be a face model.' Then she reached into her drawer and took something out. 'A going-away present,' she said, placing a small, fluted, gold container in the palm of my hand. 'Go on,' she said, 'open it up.' It was the brightest red lip colour I had ever seen, a whole new stick. 'I think you're old enough now,' she said.

You know, before that trip I'd never been to a city bigger than Birmingham, so when the plane flew down low over New York and I could see all those lights, it was the best experience of my entire life.

'Just think how much electricity lights this city up,' said Daddy, taking a long sip of his gin and tonic. Then he pointed to a tall building that I recognised from a movie. 'Look, there's the Empire State,' he said. And when I looked at that building, do you know what I thought I saw? I saw a dark shape, man-sized, floating close beside it. It was Superman come to save the day.

Thirteen years and four months old, and there I was on my first night in New York in the Apollo lounge eating French fries in a basket and a cheeseburger. It looked a bit like the Fat Joe's diner in Southampton, except that there the waitresses wore a bottle-green uniform and it didn't have a piano player.

'So how does it feel to be in the great old US of A?' Daddy said, poised to take a second large bite of his burger. It was strange talking to Dad on my own. I never saw him at home. In the evenings he would work late and at the weekends he played golf at the local club, and nothing could interfere with that. Daddy said it was good for business. Instead of talking, I began humming along to the piano. When the pianist caught me looking at him, he turned right towards me and winked, and then I studied the last few fries I wasn't going to eat.

Starters and first courses, I'll always leave a bit of, but desserts are special to me, and I remember the one I ate that night as being the most delicious I'd ever had. And just seeing it made me really realise that I was in a foreign country. Because my head was feeling a little foggy from the flying and the time difference, for a while I had forgotten where I was. They called it a banana sundae on the menu. But it wasn't served in a bowl like in England. It came in a saucepan, and the ice-cream scoops were so big that, as I was scraping the last spoonful from round the edges of the pan, I felt a heavy weight in my stomach, and then a pain like I'd just been kicked in the abdomen.

Just before we left the restaurant, Daddy went over to the piano player. He removed a few dollar bills from his wallet and placed them in the jar at the man's feet. Daddy liked to tip everyone – generously. Mum said it was because his father had been a taxi driver in the East End where no one had much money. Dad said: 'If you've got it, flaunt it!' When the piano player saw what he had done, he whispered something in Daddy's ear and Daddy called me over.

'What would you like me to play, lady?' the piano player said. I could feel my cheeks reddening and it took me a while to rearrange my thoughts. After a while I said: 'Do you know "Greensleeves"?' I don't know why I said that; it just popped into my head. It was something I used to dance to at ballet class. We'd pretend to be holding a bird in a cage and then lose it. And when he played it I remembered Mrs Summers saying, 'Smile, girls, s-m-i-l-e,' at the end, when the bird and the girl were reunited. And then I remember noticing that the piano the piano player was playing was actually a Casio keyboard as thin as the table we had just left.

What I remember about the time between New York and Denver, Colorado is a lot of travelling, because, as anyone knows who's been to America, it's a long way to go, and I suppose as much as anything I learnt how big the world is. If I remember correctly, we stayed in one city between those two places: Chicago. Things were going well for Daddy. He'd sold half a million and was going for half a million more. By day someone from the office would take me shopping or sightseeing, and by night I would sit up in bed with a tray of cheesy crackers, flipping through the quiz shows or watching some of the monster movies Daddy hadn't yet sold. Sometimes I would fall asleep before brushing my teeth, my fingers wrapped tightly around the remote control.

One night Daddy came home from the office early and asked me what I wanted to do. After a moment's thought, I said: 'The drive-in.' You see, I had fond memories of the sleep-over parties me and Claire and Stacy and Sharon and Louise had in Birmingham. What we'd do is we'd turn the *Grease* soundtrack up really high and mime to all the songs, standing on the bed in our nightgowns and singing into our shoes. We took turns being Sandy and Rizzo, the one who gets pregnant, but we all liked to be Sandy best because Sandy gets all the great songs and she turns into a real woman at the end. But what they're always doing in *Grease* is having fun at the drive-in movies, and fun was what I felt like having that night.

The drive-in was just off the second exit on the right of the turnpike. One of the men from the office Daddy was visiting had lent Daddy his car for the night. He was a little shaky at the wheel. When I was directing him right, he turned left and vice versa. 'I've got to get this car back in good shape, Lisa-Lou, so don't mess around with those directions. I'm not insured,' he said. I never knew people really drove those kind of cars in real life. It was silver and stretched out so wide at the back you could fit in a king-sized bed and still have room left over. As soon as we pulled up in our space at the Miami Movie House, Daddy took out some notes from his wallet and said to me: 'Go and get me some coffee, will you?'

The air was chilly outside and I was glad of my cardigan. We'd had no more of the storms we'd run into in New York, but it was still cloudy. The queue was long, and by the time I came out it was dark and difficult to see anything. Every silver car I came to, I would bend down and peer inside for Daddy, but it was always the wrong man.

'Hey doll, you lookin' for me?' one of them said, showing a gold-capped tooth when he grinned, and when I described the kind of car I was looking for, he said: 'Oh, you're going with that creep over there?' and pointed towards a familiar figure leaning against the boot of a car. When I walked over, Daddy said: 'Where the hell have you been?' and I said: 'There was a long queue and then I got lost.' He sighed and took a sip of coffee and opened the passenger door.

The movie was about a creature who comes out of a lagoon and spreads his green slime over entire cities. I just remember Daddy laughing a lot and saying: 'They don't make 'em like this any more.' I couldn't concentrate properly. All I had going through my head were the words the man with the gold tooth had said.

I have always taken care of my appearance – not in the way that Mummy did, going to beauty salons and all that – but I have worn full make-up every day since I was twelve. I learnt to cleanse, tone and moisturise from *Mizz* magazine, and the rest – the foundation, the eyes, the cheeks, the lips – I picked up from watching Mum. But at the age of thirteen I never thought anyone would see me as a woman. I suppose I have a large frame, that is one thing, and the curse came early, so I was tall for my age. And the suit Daddy said I was to wear must have made me look grown up.

By the time we flew into Denver, the clouds had turned to snow and the roads were blocked all the way to Glenwood Springs. Uncle Phillip had said he would try his damnedest to meet us, and he was there in the arrivals lounge at the appointed time.

'David,' he said, rushing up to Daddy and grabbing his hand. 'It's been too long. Bet you didn't recognise me, eh? Put on a few of the old barrels around the middle?'

I had no idea what kind of figure Uncle Phillip had cut before. All I knew was that he looked so bloated, a needle stuck in any part of his anatomy would make him burst. He was an inflated version of the Michelin man. He was the man in the photograph in the *Guinness Book of Records*, entitled 'Largest man alive'.

'And Lisa-Lou. I've heard so much about you,' he said, kissing me on both cheeks, leaving a small wet patch on each which, a few seconds later, I wiped off with the back of my hand. 'You've turned into such a beautiful lady! I bet the fellers all say that, don't they?'

Then he led us outside to his jeep. 'Enough room in here for seven bags more,' he said when he'd finished loading up the boot. 'Top-of-the-range Fiat, you know? Four-wheel drive'll get us through this weather. But good quality you've got to pay for, am I right, David, or am I right?' he said, nudging my father and winking at me.

Well, we had to drive ten, maybe twelve, miles to Uncle

Phillip's. He lived in a place called Welcum about twenty miles from Denver. 'We've got everything we want five minutes from our own front door,' explained Uncle Phillip. 'School, bank, post office, wellness centre, golf course. You still teeing up, David?'

Auntie Marlene and my cousins were waiting on the driveway when we pulled up. And even though it was the middle of April it felt like Christmas all over again. Their house was as pretty as a greetings card. Snow covered the roof in perfect curves, like it had been painted on with glitter, and there were pink-coloured shutters on each window.

'You've travelled such a long way,' said Auntie Marlene, hugging us both. 'You must be so tired,' she said. Once we were inside, the maid relieved us of our bags. 'The blue room for David and the white room for the girl,' Auntie Marlene said, and the maid disappeared upstairs. Then Auntie Marlene smiled at me. 'Lisa-Lou, there's a bathroom just here if you want to freshen up before dinner,' she said.

Have you ever seen one of those costume dramas, those TV adaptations of Charles Dickens, for example, or William Shakespeare? Well, they always have a room, a grand dining-room, where the guests sit down at a long oak table – so long that they are spaced so far apart they couldn't touch one another even if they tried. Well, that is what the dining-room in Uncle Phillip's house was like. And the food – it was as if we were eating in a restaurant. As we were finishing dessert, Auntie Marlene said: 'You know, I just can't get over how like your mother you are, Lisa-Lou. Spitting image, isn't she, Phillip? The same eyes.'

'The resemblance is remarkable,' said Uncle Phillip, 'quite remarkable.'

When I was a child I had blonde hair, and my mother always said to my father: 'How did we produce this child, David, you with your red hair and me with my brunette?' Neighbours called me the little angel, because that's what I looked like. Rosy red cheeks and cherubic grin. But as I got older, the blonde became brown and my complexion paler, and by the time I was ten years old, people would confuse photos of me with those of my mother at the same age.

'Nothing like our little ones. You wouldn't have thought they were related,' Auntie Marlene said. Duane and Mike looked like the clean, presentable children you meet in a Great Universal Stores catalogue, faces so perfect they shined as if they'd just been polished.

'Your accent is funny,' Duane said, looking right at me.

'Duane,' Auntie Marlene said. 'Don't be so rude. Lisa-Lou has a lovely English accent. After dessert, you can go get your Superman costume to show her.'

'You said it would be just like in the movies, but it's not. She doesn't say thaaanks, she says thiinks,' Duane said, banging the end of his fork on the table.

Easter Day, and there were chocolate eggs the size of hens waiting beside our breakfast plates. They were all tied up with pink ribbon and pieces of silver string, and when I separated the two half shells I found a small plastic bag inside containing miniature eggs. Duane and Mike were already on to their second egg and it was only nine fifteen.

'Try yours, Lisa-Lou,' they shouted, touching the box of my egg with their sticky fingers.

'I want to eat my breakfast first,' I said, pouring some milk on to my cereal.

'Have you seen Daddy's?' they said, pointing to a large box in the corner. 'It was the biggest one in the store.' If our eggs were hen-sized, Uncle Phillip's was as big as an ostrich. The box was so large it reached the waist of the eldest boy. 'Mummy told me off for using it as a chair,' he said, 'but the box is really strong, look,' and he prodded it with his finger.

After breakfast I took a walk in the garden. I was nearing the clematis when I heard a shrill voice say: 'Lisa-Lou, look who's come to save you!' and when I turned round there was Duane running towards me in an all-in-one blue and red jumpsuit, cape trailing behind and arms stuck out in front.

'Lisa-Lou,' he said. 'Lisa-Lou, let's play a game. Let's pretend you're a lady who's been tied up by the Joker, and Superman comes and saves you.'

'Duane, I've got it,' said Mike, running towards us with a ball of string, the kind you use to tie up plants that aren't growing properly. And then it seemed that as soon as I had muttered a begrudging OK, my hands were being tied up to the trellis, secured by the kind of knots only Scouts know how to do.

Well, I waited and waited, and before long I realised that the boys had been gone more than a quarter of an hour. I knew this because the string pulled at my sleeve in such a way that, if I lowered my head and slightly craned it to the right, I could just see the minute hand of my watch.

You know sometimes when you've waited all evening to see a programme on TV? You've got your tray of hot chocolate and crackers and cheese or whatever you like to nibble, and you've settled down in your favourite armchair, two plump cushions positioned so that the arm-rest does not dig into your shoulder blades. But then you turn on the TV, and what do you see? A football match that has gone into extra time. A documentary about an actor, recently deceased. An extended news bulletin. And you realise that, for one reason or another, your favourite programme has been cancelled due to unforeseen circumstances. For a moment, your heart quickens and you feel the blood drain away to a place deep inside yourself. You think: they've betrayed me. I've been betrayed. But then, after a few minutes, you get on with doing something else, like flicking through a magazine, and you forget about it. With my relatives, my expectations had been dashed and there was no such escape. I had three more days at their house.

And after pondering this for a while, I thought of all those movies I'd seen. The girl gets tied up and the only way she can break free is by finding a man to rescue her or by forcing herself to loosen the ties. Well, as I knew there was no prospect of anyone coming to that quiet corner of the garden, the only thing I could do was move my hands up and down the trellis to try and weaken the string. And, sure enough, the sawing motion gradually paid off: the string became thinner and thinner and within ten minutes I was running over the grass, wrists red raw, shouting the names of my cousins.

I found them in the garage. They didn't see me because it

was dark inside and they seemed to be preoccupied. I bent my knees a little, because I guessed that the more I showed of my face, the more likely they were to notice me. The window was a little frosty, but I did not want to risk clearing it with my fingernail in case they heard it tap-tapping on the glass. As well as the Chevrolet, the garage was home to any number of gardening appliances. Shears of different sizes hung on the walls and there was a mower, the kind that looks like a small tractor, in one corner. The younger child was raised up higher than the other one, and on occasions he would reach under his chair for something. The third time he did this I saw that the chair he was sitting on was actually a box, and that the stuff he was removing from it was brown and stained his hands. He passed some of this stuff to his brother – face blushing as red as his cape – and crammed a whole chunk of the gift in his mouth.

It was my duty to inform, and I did not feel especially guilty about doing so, considering my treatment at the hands of those boys. So when I was striding across the lawn towards the house, my mind was on other things, and it could only have been sheer luck that I spotted, from the corner of my eye, something large and writhing on the patio. At first, I thought it was one of the neighbourhood dogs playing idly with a ball. But when I grew closer I saw that the convulsions were not those of a paw tensing and groping, but of a human arm in spasm for no apparent reason.

The ambulance didn't arrive for quarter of an hour. It took three men to lift Uncle Phillip on to the stretcher. You couldn't see his face because it was bandaged up with a tea towel to stop the blood flowing from his head. It had taken a nasty knock when he'd collapsed on the patio. Auntie Marlene could only say: 'It was the egg. He couldn't find his Easter egg and he got crazy about it.'

He'd had heart problems before, my father told me that evening, and a neighbour – who had seen the ambulance and was concerned – told us that her husband, a doctor, had warned Uncle Phillip five years ago that he should be cutting down his calorie intake by two-thirds. But Uncle Phillip was a stubborn character, and still he ate his chocolate and ice-cream and fry-up breakfasts and enjoyed his sedentary lifestyle.

We visited him only once. He was in a room of his own. Quite white it was. He could not speak when we saw him. He was lying prone, eyes closed. His face seemed to have aged twenty years. It was ashen, the colour of meat left too long out of the fridge. His hands were resting on his chest, and the flesh there was so translucent I thought that, if you looked carefully, you could see his bones. For a while we just sat there at either side of the bed, without saying a word to each other or to Uncle Phillip. The only sound was the occasional beep-beep of the monitor, a small red dot sweeping along a screen from left to right, its trail marking the highs and lows of Uncle Phillip's heart.

'You should talk to him, it's good for his brain,' said the nurse. So we did what we could. Daddy talked about the weather. How it was getting better now. The thaw was on, but he shouldn't worry about it because it was slow and there wouldn't be any burst pipes. He told him about his success with the Denver executives – selling two blockbusters in twenty-four hours. But

I couldn't say a thing. Because while Daddy was talking, I was watching the red dot rise and fall, in time with the movements of Uncle Phillip's chest, and I thought, what really matters are the things inside, the things beyond the surface, things even Florence Nightingale cannot control.

A few days later we were travelling to San Francisco for our return flight, when we stopped overnight in a place just on the edge of the desert. Early in the morning I went to explore. I wore only shorts and a T-shirt; even at six the sun was so strong I could not bear my suit. I knew in my heart that it was dangerous to leave without a map but, all holiday, I had wanted to feel sand on my feet, and now that I had the opportunity I was not going to pass it by.

The sand I expected was the light-brown stuff, with grains that get caught between your toes and stay there for days. But the sand I saw had formed in rocks, dense gatherings of grains that stuck together hard and did not break. As I walked on this ground, I was reminded of all the things I had experienced on the trip that had not been what I expected.

And then I noticed something shiny on the sand – a new coin. I picked it up, and I knew that I did this because of my father. You see, whenever he spotted money on the ground, he'd whip it up as fast as he could and pop it in his pocket before anyone saw, and then he'd say: 'See a penny, pick it up, all the day you'll have good luck,' just so we'd know what he'd done. But when I looked at this coin carefully, I realised that it was larger than our penny and that the face on it was not that of Florence Nightingale, but of a man I did not recognise. I held it up level with my eye to get a closer look. What my eye saw was not the frown on his face or his grimace, but the reflection of my hair, which had been bleached as blonde as an angel's. Then I tossed the coin aside and walked on.

Woman's Best Friend | David Croft

I called in on Jo and asked her how she'd been this past while since the accident. She said she was fine and that I shouldn't have bothered calling. She says this every week as her faculties aren't quite what they used to be, so she never remembers when I've called from one week to the next. But it was no trouble, I assured her, not least that it was partially my fault that she was in this state in the first place. Well, how was I to know she was going to be in the attic when I set fire to it? It was that festering old bastard McGlinchy that I was after. Apparently she was too.

Judge McGlinchy was a mean old git who took pleasure in making sure that no one else in life had any. Strictly speaking, he wasn't a judge at all as he'd retired years ago. In fact, I can't actually ever remember him being a judge. Even if he had of been, I can't imagine he would have been very fair as he wasn't very fair to any of the townsfolk.

You see, Judge McGlinchy killed my dog. On purpose. As it transpired, he killed Jo Welton's dog too, and Mary Mac's dog, and Robbie Flowers'. I don't wish to sound callous, but their dogs were all mongrels, whereas mine was a pedigree boxer. Amber was his name. A fine liver colour with a white face and socks. I'd been given him as a Christmas present, by my folks, when I was eight.

If I'd known McGlinchy had killed other folks' dogs too, I would have formed a gang or a committee or something. Instead we all went our own separate ways trying to get revenge on the old man. Jo and myself were the only ones to survive.

I accidentally killed Mary Mac when, early one morning, I wired up McGlinchy's door handle to the pylon in his back yard. My dad worked for the Electricity Board and showed me how to re-wire most things that needed a current. Though pylons weren't one of them. But once you've wired a transistor radio up to your bedroom door handle to stop your kid brother invading your space, well . . . it's the same principle really.

I'd just finished connecting up the jump leads and was making my way round to the front of the house to knock on the door when I heard a muffled bang. Mary Mac had got there before me with a twelve-gauge shotgun. She was going to shoot the old bastard for killing her dog, Sabre. As you can imagine, she wasn't about to knock. She marched right up the porch steps and grabbed the door handle. The shock blew her clean across the street into Mr Kovak's privets.

Men had to come wearing rubber suits to remove the body so's she wouldn't electrocute them. Electrocuting people wasn't uncommon to Mary Mac, though, as she used to be a nurse up at the asylum and electrocuted people practically every day. That's why she kept Sabre. It was a cross between a Doberman and a Rottweiler with a little sabre-toothed tiger thrown in for good measure. She kept him as a guard dog just in case any of the ex-inmates found out where she lived. She would sit out on the porch with a shotgun in her lap and Sabre by her side, and if anyone passed on her side of the street, Sabre would run down to the fence and rip chunks of wood off to try and get at them.

One day, as luck would have it, McGlinchy was walking down Crozier Avenue, on his way to meet one of his spurious gentlemen friends no doubt, when Sabre caught sight of him and bolted down to the fence howling and frothing. The fence had become so worn over the years that Sabre tore one of the struts clean off and was trying to get through the hole he'd just created to tear another hole in old McGlinchy. Mary Mac panicked, ran down to the fence and began pulling at Sabre's tail, all the while shouting obscenities at McGlinchy. Meanwhile, at the other end, Sabre wasn't about to let go of McGlinchy's cashmere even though the old man was beating him over the head with a walking cane. Sabre would growl then yelp, growl then yelp.

It was due to the sound of her dog in such distress that Mary Mac pulled with a little more vigour and, in doing so, fell backwards, discharging both barrels of the shotgun, which she had tucked under her arm, right up Sabre's backside.

The police questioned McGlinchy about why he would go to such extraordinary lengths to kill Mary Mac, but decided to release him when they realised he only had one foot and would never of been able to climb a sixty-foot pylon.

David Croft

He said he'd lost his foot during the war; the Germans had cut it off because he kept trying to escape. But my grandad said that he had deliberately shot himself in the foot so he wouldn't have to take part in the Battle of the Bulge, and that it had gone septic by the time the German medics found him hiding in a trench under the bodies of his fellow soldiers.

I, meanwhile, kept quiet about my involvement in the incident. Firstly because I hadn't meant to kill Mary Mac, and secondly because she was as spooky as old McGlinchy. I did feel bad about my dad though. They questioned him and a few other engineers who had the expertise to rig up such an elaborate execution, but, luckily for him, a pimp and a hooker came forward to verify his alibi.

Robbie Flowers was a different story altogether. He was only ten at the time, and very good at soccer I seem to remember. In fact, he used to play soccer with his dog, Pele. Pele the dog bore no resemblance to Pele the player apart from the fact that he was black. He would probably have been better off being called Gordon Banks, as he was a much more accomplished goalkeeper. Robbie would blast shots from twenty yards, curl them, chip them, and every time, this hybrid springer cum Labrador would jump up and block the ball.

It was during one of these training sessions that Pele came to grief. Robbie had just unleashed a 25-yard volley which Pele athletically tipped over the crossbar into McGlinchy's back yard. Without hesitation, Pele scrambled through a hole in the fence to retrieve the ball. Before he got within ten feet of it, a shot cracked out from the back door of the house and

Pele somersaulted over himself, collapsing in a bloody heap in the rose bushes.

Robbie, as you can imagine, was so hysterical that he ran through the same hole in the fence, stooping to pick up a lump of wood as he did so. McGlinchy, oblivious to the child, retreated into the house. As all this was going on I was furiously tugging at a series of ropes and pulleys that were connected to a woodcutter's axe which I had suspended above the door.

My plan had been: boy knocks on door, boy runs away, man opens door, boy pulls on rope, man gets axe in head, Amber is avenged.

But would the axe come down? McGlinchy was there for ages, lining up his hunting rifle on poor old Pele. I was pulling and tugging, all to no avail. When he went back into the house I stopped. It was then that I saw Robbie running up the back steps wielding his four by two. It seemed like that axe took five years to fall. When it did come down it came with such a gristly, crunching thud that all I could think about was Amber's jowly face being squashed into a waste disposal unit.

Later, McGlinchy claimed that he'd shot the dog in self defence, as it had gone completely mad and would have torn his throat out if he hadn't put it out of its misery.

The cops seemed to accept this, albeit with a little suspicion. My dad wasn't quite so lucky though. They wanted to know why an axe with his initials on it had been used to try and kill McGlinchy, and indisputedly used to kill young Robbie Flowers. Dad didn't have much of an explanation for this so the cops took him away. I vowed to myself that I would confess to the crime

David Croft

after I'd got my revenge on McGlinchy. But that was the last I ever saw of him. Unfortunately Dad died of syphilis before I could honour my promise.

I don't suppose you can really blame old McGlinchy for killing Sabre, but you can for Amber and Pele, and you most definitely can for Jo's dog, Mitsy.

Jo was out walking her toy poodle cum Yorkshire terrier. The cold November snow had left a shroud over the manicured gardens and a wafer-thin layer of ice over the pond. It was while she was admiring the patterns in the ice that she noticed McGlinchy on the far side trying to extricate something from the inside of his new cashmere coat. Now, if there was one thing Mitsy liked it was sticks and swimming; McGlinchy knew this and promptly threw a stick right into the middle of the pond. Mitsy duly jumped in to retrieve it, much to the protestations of Jo. What you couldn't see from her side of the pond was the cat gut and fish hooks that were wrapped around the stick. Once poor old Mitsy sank her teeth into the stick, the fish hooks sank themselves into her jaw. McGlinchy then proceeded to pick up a large stone that lay at his feet, which coincidentally had the other end of the cat gut tied around it, and threw it into the pond. The stone sank, and moments later so did Mitsy, albeit with more of a struggle.

It was rumoured that he committed this hideous deed in retaliation for Jo not supplying him with the sexual favours that she once had. It was also rumoured that she undertook these favours in order to keep her husband out of prison. But since her husband was dead, so was any obligation she felt to McGlinchy.

In some ways I was glad that her husband was dead because I'd always had a crush on her. I thought that someday, even though she was much older than me, she would fall in love with me and we could run away and get married. I wrote her a letter once professing my undying love, which she thought was so charming. She said she was very flattered and that I was too nice for her and that I should find someone my own age as she would be an old hag by the time I was twenty-one. She giggled a lot when she read it; then she gave me a big hug, ruffled my hair and kissed me on the cheek.

I was so embarrassed that for months after I used to cycle the long way to school, through the cemetery, past the disused lumber yard. Secretly, though, I think she liked me, because when it came around to my twelfth birthday she sent me a card which read: 'Hope you have a wonderful birthday, Love Jo.' I kept the card under my pillow; at night I'd take it out and press the ink to my lips. I imagined I was kissing her fingers, her lips, her eyes, her long red hair, even her nose. I stopped after a while, though, as it went all smudgy and was getting difficult to read.

I used to lie awake at night and stare at the ceiling, trying not to imagine what she did with McGlinchy. I'd tell myself she wasn't that kind of woman. She was caring and gentle. I dreamt that we lay together in her bed. And she would hold me and kiss me, not on the cheek but on the mouth. I never thought of us making love, she was too nice for that. Don't get me wrong, I fantasised about having sex with other girls all the time, but that was different. I didn't love them.

I imagined that she fell so much in love with me that she sold her house, packed up the car and drove us both to Mexico, where we lived in a wooden house on stilts by the sea. I thought this was a really romantic idea, but it was also partly to do with the fact that my mum would totally flip if we lived together in town.

In reality, my plans for eternal bliss were a little premature, seeing as her husband had only been dead for six weeks.

Pierse, Jo's husband, had committed suicide after auditors began to uncover a certain misappropriation of his accountancy firm's funds. (Apparently he misappropriated about half a million.) McGlinchy, being the town's ex-judge, convinced Jo that, if she scratched his back so to speak, he would get Judge Barmby to throw the case out of court on a technicality. For the life of me, I couldn't understand why she agreed to this, because if she hadn't, it meant Pierse would go to jail and we could be together for the rest of our lives. It was that kind of unselfishness that made me love her even more.

The rest of the townsfolk thought that Pierse had found out about their liaison and shot himself in disgust. In fact it was because he was totally oblivious to the affair but had been blackmailed by McGlinchy, thus losing most of the money he had stolen in the first place.

A few weeks after losing Mitsy, her last remaining family member, Jo decided to pay old McGlinchy a visit, under the pretence of patching things up. Being the perverted old bastard that he was, he agreed.

Judge McGlinchy's sexual habits were no mystery to the town. He wasn't fussy if he had men or women, boys or girls. Some say he even dabbled with animals, on account of Farmer Jackson finding most of his chickens had been killed in some bizarre sexual ritual a few years back.

No one ever challenged McGlinchy about his sexual exploits, primarily because he did most of them in the neighbouring towns, and secondly because he had all of the local law enforcement so stitched up with evidence of corruption and illicit activities that none of them would dare stand up against him.

One night, in December I recall, he took Jo up to his attic where he kept an array of masks, whips, chains, and all sorts of other instruments of sexual torture. Her plan was to handcuff him to his replica electric chair, as she had done on so many other occasions, but instead of donning her peaked Nazi cap and doing whatever it was she normally did to him, she would cut off his genitals and asphyxiate him with them.

It was at this point that I arrived on the scene. I had become so frustrated with my ingeniously elaborate plans to kill McGlinchy that I decided on a more direct approach.

I'd gone to the garage at home, pulled back the dustsheet on Dad's old Buick, and siphoned off what petrol was left in it. I filled up two lemonade bottles and stuffed one of Dad's handkerchiefs into the neck of each one.

From my position up the old oak tree in McGlinchy's front garden, the only room I could see with a light on and any activity was the attic. So I lit one of my Molotov cocktails and tossed it through the window. I scrambled down the tree and lobbed the other one through a window in the front door.

I watched for a while from a safe distance behind Kovak's privets. I was so excited I almost wet myself. At last, Amber would be avenged. Burnt to death! A fitting end for the man who had killed my dog by forcing his head into a waste disposal unit just for crapping on his rose bushes. Kovak said that McGlinchy had beaten Amber senseless with a broom while he was still in the act, then he dragged him into the house and Amber was never seen again.

Of course, I didn't have any proof about the waste disposal part, but for weeks later his drains sure did stink. And I found what looked suspiciously like one of Amber's floppy brown and white ears in his trash can.

After about five or ten minutes the fire had really taken; there was no way anybody could survive the inferno that had a hold on that old tinderbox. But, to my horror, I could see someone moving around in the hallway. A few moments later Jo emerged from the front door with her rubber jackboots and plastic basque melting to her skin. I vaulted the privets, ran across the street, up the drive and threw myself on top of her to smother the flames. The plastic was sticking to my hands and setting my parka on fire too. I rolled her around in the damp night grass until eventually I must have passed out.

When Judge Barmby asked me why I had killed his fellow judge in such a macabre manner, I didn't know what to say. I looked over at Jo sitting in her wheelchair, bandaged from head to toe, unable to talk. I just told him it was because I loved her.

I got twenty five years for arson, grievous bodily harm and murder.

I'm thirty-seven now and visit Jo once or twice a week; she's fifty-eight and has spent the past few years in Mary Mac's old place.

Jacaranda | Angus Calder

Mr Mackenzie's light, precise voice thrilled her.

'Mrs Leslie? I am very pleased to be able to inform you that I have made enquiries about Mr Kariuki and his activities. He is a sound man. I am told that his credit is good. As you know, nothing is one hundred per cent certain in this country just now. But I think you can sell your house to him with *reasonable* safety.'

So there it was . . . Merchiston would be sold. She trusted her bank manager. Like her he came from Edinburgh. Since Kariuki was sound, she would meet him at the lawyers' tomorrow and sign things. That would be *it*, over.

She put the phone down with thrill separating into two feelings: relief and panic. Ten thirty was early for a gin, but she needed a gin and tonic.

She carried it out to the verandah, sat in her old cane chair, couldn't take everything in. Back to Scotland in just a few weeks. On one of those jet planes. November or December. It would be cold.

Here the sun would shine almost every day, as now. She could hear the sprinkler swishing on the lawn in front of Merchiston. She could hear Karanja hoeing. In Scotland these had been summer sounds only.

She'd settle in Spain. Gladys had told her Spain was warm and cheap. Gladys said there were fine new flats on the south coast of Spain somewhere, now she'd forgotten the name of the place.

Margaret didn't like Britain any more. It was cold and expensive and that man Wilson had let in lots of black foreigners. There were those boys with guitars and long hair; what were they called – Wasps, or Slaters? No, Beetles. They were just noisy, yet Gladys said even her mother loved them. Sheer noise.

On her last trip to Edinburgh, taking Sheila to leave her in digs, it had been Festival time, and the city was full of dirty young people with ugly accents and ugly clothes. It hadn't seemed like her native city – a strange, ugly place. The country she loved to read about, in her favourite Victorian novels; that England, too, that had gone.

The dew had long since dried. The garden was sad under the heavy sun. That pale, dull, high equatorial sky had hung over her last thirty-five years. That coarse grass over the red earth would cut you if you didn't cut it first. Her flowers were making very little show. They were nicer first thing and in the evening. The bougainvillaea hedge was a poisonous, wicked fairy-tale red. At the far end, across the watercourse, behind the mango and avocado trees, Jack Smedley's little estate had been bought by a swarming African clan, with a shabby granny in a wool cap and about six piccaninnies in various sizes of school uniform, mostly fitting them.

Oh yes, it was time to leave Kenya.

She would have another gin. No one to stop her. Alec was dead. Rose had finished cleaning, gone to town, with Joseph. And Joseph would be hours yet, buying what might be her last load of basic groceries for Merchiston, getting that noise in the car seen to before she sold it.

On the bookcase beside the drinks cabinet, the photographs struck her and for a moment she wanted to cry. That G & S production in which she and Alec had met. Him as Ko Ko, she as Yum Yum. He'd been so young for that part, just a junior hospital doctor, yet everyone had agreed he did the patter song best. And she'd been happy, a little maid just out of school herself, not a care in the world. Then, more than twenty years later ('What a handsome couple they make,' she'd heard people had often said), herself and Alec dressed for golf with their clubs, looking elegant, still young, smiling, and little Sheila with her little club scowling away from the camera, wearing a tammy.

There had been good times here. More G & S, though Alec went off it, she never understood why; tennis (he'd left her to it in what he called 'your set'; golf (rarely with him); bridge, at which he was so fierce. And so many good parties, outside on evenings neither sticky with heat nor cold, moving inside when you felt the chill of night on the high plateau.

With the second gin, she found the garden different. She'd got so used to the jacaranda there, in the corner. She'd let its blue just merge with sky and dust. Now it suddenly seemed preciously beautiful. A hawk – a kite, they called them, so odd – flew low and slowly above the tree. Those new neighbours kept chickens. Its head, fine-cut, chivalric, turned slowly, peering down. Blue trumpets of jacaranda sounded for this knight pricking across the plain of the sky.

As she lit her fifth cigarette, her eyes filled with tears. She would miss Kenya. Her home. For so long. Thirty-five years. Another drink.

On the escritoire, as she went to the cabinet, Sheila's letter. Sheila's hateful letter. Now she could face reading it properly. She picked it up – two clumsily, closely typed sides of one of those blue airmail things, interrupted by the Queen's head and the address: 'Mrs M. Leslie'. Shouldn't a child say 'Margaret'? It was all wrong.

Back on the verandah, she found her reading glasses:

'Dear Mummy' . . . (didn't children say 'Dearest'?) 'I'm sorry I really can't come to Daddy's funeral. Even if I could afford it, which I *can't*, I wouldn't want to, even if you paid my fare. I loved Daddy very much and have cried buckets since I heard. He was a very kind man, I now see this very clearly. Did he ever tell you about all those African children he treated free? But I couldn't stand meeting those men who'd all be there, those red-faced "chaps" from his club, his cricketing pals, golfers, and those snooty consultants from the hospital. I know how it would be. First of all they'd disapprove of me and make sarky comments, whatever I was wearing. Then –

you bet your life! – they'd start pawing at me, trying to take me aside, breathing whisky all over me. That sort of thing began when I was thirteen. I used to tell Daddy. He laughed me out of it . . .'

Told her father. Never Mummy. Never Margaret.
She lit her sixth cigarette, screwed up her eyes, which were tearful again, read balefully on.

'I'm still enjoying the Uni. I'm going to do Honours History. There are lecturers here who know about African history, and one of them's been very nice to me. It's great to sit in a big library finding out all the lies they taught me at that school.'

The best in the colony, thank you, miss. You were privileged. Not to speak of the horrible pain of your birth, the end of pleasure with Alec in bed . . .

'Kamau wrote to me recently. He's in London, doing engineering. He's got married somehow – a woman from Ghana, he says. He's very serious these days. All work, no play, he says.'

Kamau . . . Despite the gin, Margaret felt threatened, angry. Kamau was at the bottom of all this unnatural hatefulness.
Oh yes, Alec had told her about the African children. She'd said, 'That's jolly good of you, dear.' She'd thought, well, if

that's how he feels he must spend his time . . . It seemed like the sort of Christian thing doctors had to do – though most didn't. She'd actually approved of the high rates he paid to servants. Joseph, she felt, was rather special, with qualities you found in Victorian novels. Knowing about this side of Alec hadn't prepared her for that afternoon, just four years ago.

She'd been in town, lunching with Gladys and Celia at the New Stanley and buying, for that big party, some of the special things you couldn't ask Joseph to buy. (Poor man. Once when she'd listed cocktail cherries he'd come back with a jar of onions. Celia had joked rather cruelly that if she'd asked for gherkins he'd have come back with turtle soup.) When she'd parked in the drive she'd heard voices on the verandah and, leaving Joseph to carry in the boxes by the side way, had gone round to the back.

And what did she see! Alec was telling a long story in that funny thick Dundee accent of his which he saved for stories. She remembered his grizzled, curly head with its neat moustache and large grey eyes gleaming and creased with that pleasure he showed when he was relaxed and happy. There was Sheila, on holiday from school, in her neat white tennis shoes and skirt, with that lovely deep tan of hers setting off her neat fair hair.

And there, drinking a beer, was Kamau.

She'd tried to smile, said 'Good afternoon', panicked, muttered something about 'things in the kitchen' and rushed through, head down. Joseph had left the boxes on the kitchen table for her and gone. She'd stood in a blaze of fear and begun noisily taking out jars and cans. Cherries. Tinned shellfish. Gherkins. Clatter. Chunk. She was angry.

'What's *this*, Margaret?' Alec's face in the doorway was grim, the laugh-lines converted to fissures as if in rock.

'Oh, this party . . .'

'No, it's *not* the party. You were quite amazingly rude out there. Sheila brings home a friend and . . .'

'*Friend?*'

'Yes, a friend.'

'Where, pray, does she get *friends* like that?'

'In what they call a discothèque, she tells me. He's a student at the college. He's a clever young man.'

'Well, he may be . . .'

Now, sipping her gin, the jacaranda blurred by her reading glasses, the garden dull under midday sun, the kite departed, Margaret still felt vibrate inside her the outrageous image of Kamau. Fuzzy, curling hair, not barbered like Joseph's, just sort of chopped into. Not a real beard – particles of hair on cheek and chin. Big lips and huge eyes in a round face. She imagined his smell. Dirt, woodsmoke and sweat. That's what Africans smelt of. His T-shirt and jeans, those sloppy clothes he wore, would be soaked in dirt and sweat.

And his people. Those terrible oaths to kill all the whites. Bestial Mau Mau rites. The murders.

She'd thought Kenyatta a monster, swearing that oath. Now Gladys told her that these days he was all right. The best man to lead. Quite charming to her when she'd gone to that party at State House. Maybe times did change. But not that image of Kamau.

She'd said to Alec, there, in the kitchen: 'I think you are

a monster. Your own daughter. A man like that. She's so
vulnerable. Don't you see? This country?'

Then Sheila's voice behind her had cut in: 'Oh no I'm not,
Mummy.'

And that was why Sheila still hated her. Why she wouldn't
come to the funeral. Now, how could she meet her in Edinburgh?
How could she drop this hate?

In fact, because it had gone wrong, the funeral might have
suited Sheila. There had been a big turnout. Yes, the red-faced
cricketers and doddery golfers had been there, and the white
medical colleagues, and people she'd never thought of coming,
like the Frenchman who ran that restaurant and the Greek man
who was a dentist or something. And Asian businessmen – well,
some of them were quite charming and she'd never deny that.
But also Africans – young doctors and students. One of Kamau's
friends came with a young doctor. He was smarter than Kamau,
this Mwangi – all suit and shine.

She'd never imagined it. Gladys, and her Sam, with whom
she'd discussed all the arrangements, just hadn't brought up this
possibility. And when Sam had said at the graveside very loudly:
'Mrs Leslie thanks you all for coming and invites you all . . .'
she couldn't object, couldn't say what she really wanted.

The few Asians who came didn't touch alcohol and left soon.
But Mwangi and his doctor friend stayed, with the cricketers
and the golfers, and the conversation became heated. Sam
wasn't worried. 'It's all right, Margaret. It's OK, Margaret,
they are good lads.' Celia had agreed with her; this wasn't
right. But Sam and Gladys couldn't see her point of view

until Sam finally said: 'Get some rest, Margaret, I'll see to things.'

In her room, more than an hour later, with her head pounding painfully, she'd heard car doors slam in the dark drive and Mwangi's voice, high-pitched, incomprehensible, still declaiming. A journalist. Gladys told her a few days later that he'd written a nice piece mentioning Alec. She never read that paper herself. She'd ignored the cutting when Gladys passed it to her. It was still in its envelope.

Back to the drinks cabinet. Back to the escritoire. Then, almost knocking her cane chair over as she sat down again, she opened the envelope.

'This column rarely has much to say for the Settlers who, let's face it, never wanted to give up their ill-gotten power. The Spiritual Home of most of them was Pretoria. But now it raises its glass in memory of one decent man, Dr Alec Leslie, who gave thirty' (it was thirty-five) 'years of his life to healing the sick of any and every race, colour and creed. A true Nation Builder, his sudden heart attack leaves many of us sad and grieving. We remember his favourite motto – "We are all Jack Thompson's bairns." Alec – goodbye.'

What he actually did say often was: 'We're all Jock Tamson's bairns.' It was a badly written, lying article. It made her feel sullied.

She was crying again, as small shadows crept from the trees, as a tiny sunbird, flashing brilliance from its scalp, darted past the verandah.

Cigarettes. Just one left. Joseph wouldn't be back till at least four thirty. Cigarettes. How to get cigarettes?

Karanja. He could go to the *duka* down the hill. Sportsman cigarettes were all right. Alec had smoked them. She couldn't walk a mile down the hill, not in this state, not even with the Alsatian. Karanja could go.

Unsteadily, banging her hip on the table, she went through the kitchen into the back yard. In fifteen years of living at Merchiston she had never really explored the servants' quarters. She had left negotiations there to Joseph; sometimes to Alec if matters were serious or Joseph were visiting his wife in the Rift Valley. But she knew which of the doors in the long bungaloid building was Karanja's. It was the one that didn't belong to Rose or Joseph.

Across the red dust, under the dusty mango tree, she stumbled to Karanja's door.

She knocked. No answer.

'*Jambo!*' she called, aware of her voice as a bray, not her own voice, a braying voice. 'Kar – an – jaa!'

No answer. She pushed at the doorknob. She fell in.

The barking of the chained dog woke her up.

As she tried to make sense of mango tree and mid-afternoon sky, the doorway was suddenly blotted out.

Quite a tall person. A woman. White eyes and teeth in a round head leant towards her.

'Memsahib?'

'Who . . . ?'

'Memsahib. Oh, I am sorry. I am Agnes, memsahib. I am Mr Karanja's niece.'

Agnes? The name at least was familiar. It had cropped up when Alec had talked to Karanja, at the side door in the evening, or when the elderly man had approached respectfully as they stepped out to their car. 'A bit of bother with one of old Karanja's relatives' was as much as Alec had ever said.

Margaret's head had fallen against a metal drum containing some sort of flour or meal. She could dimly see, in a room which would have served as a cupboard at most in the Edinburgh of her maidenhood, the brazier on which Karanja cooked. The space reeked of smoke, of decaying vegetable smells and farinaceous odours. Karanja slept in a separate similar space which could just be discerned past the brazier. On a shelf above her, Margaret now saw half a pineapple, its exposed veins browning, which explained a further tang.

Agnes was helping her up. 'Oh dear, memsahib. I am sorry you are very ill. I think you need my shoulder.'

Uncomprehending, Margaret let Agnes manipulate her so that the girl's strong neck and shoulders supported her right arm. Her fingers, sliding under the girl's shirt, felt Agnes's collar bone and bicep. Agnes slowly led her back to her own kitchen, with its different smells.

'The living-room,' Margaret managed to say, indicating with her stagger where that was.

On her sofa, Margaret began to grasp the situation. Agnes,

who stood very erect before her, hands clasped respectfully in front of her waist, was dressed in a maroon school blazer. It was frayed and faded but Margaret recognised the badge of a well-known boarding school. The girl's pleated navy frock was neat. She had smelt of dust, yes. What Margaret had smelt under the dust, as Agnes had supported her, had been soap – not bad soap, not carbolic soap.

The girl must be eighteen or nineteen at least. She was well built. That skin which looked almost shiny had, Margaret now sensed rather than remembered, a curious matt feel, like cardboard or biscuits. Though her hair was as short as a boy's, the concern in Agnes's bright eyes was womanlike. But she restrained it with politeness.

'Let me make you some tea, please, memsahib.'

Margaret half shuddered and said, 'No, no thank you.'

Joseph knew how to make tea properly but when, once or twice, on safari, Alec had insisted they accept the hospitality of African farmers, the tea had been made with hot milk poured straight on the leaves. She had had to force a little of it down.

'I would like to help you very much. Bwana Leslie was such a good man. I am like his orphan.'

Margaret nodded her head in acknowledgement. There was no headache yet, but she sensed a bruise beginning to form where her hair must have struck the can.

'He was so good to me. Did you know that? Did you know how good he was to me?'

A horrific thought was dismissed. Alec would never . . .

'No, I didn't know, How nice. How . . . very nice.'

'He paid for my schooling. Now I will go to university next year. Every day in my prayers I thank Bwana Doctor Leslie. Now I want to help you, memsahib.'

'Where . . . where is . . . your uncle?'

'I thought he would be at home.' Agnes had dropped her eyelids. 'I told him I would come to thank him today. I expect he is in that bar he goes to.'

She looked up shyly, pleadingly, confused by her mistake. 'He is not a bad man, memsahib. Since my father died, he has been my father.'

'Well, Agnes' – Margaret now felt reassured that she was herself in charge – 'you *can* help me. Thank you. I went to see your uncle because I have no cigarettes. I want cigarettes. If I give you two *shillingi*, will you go to the shop at the foot of the hill and buy cigarettes for me, please? Sportsman. They will do.'

'Sportman. Oh. Yes, memsahib.' Agnes could not sound eager or conceal her disappointment. As she left she said, 'Oh, Bwana Doctor Leslie was such a good man. I am very glad I can help you, memsahib. I thank God.'

Now Margaret found she was shaking. She couldn't remember if she'd said 'Goodbye' or 'Thank you, Agnes'. She went slowly to the bathroom and looked at herself. Grey hair, dishevelled. Her parting messed over. Eyes old and bleared. The mouth clamped. She did not like this strange woman at all. Still shaking, she pulled at her hair. The bruise was just visible. She washed her hands, thought of having a shower.

Then she'd be defenceless. Only the chained dog to guard her.

Alec had kept a loaded pistol in the escritoire drawer. She went back, checked. The key was on the mantelshelf. The pistol was still in the drawer.

She would shower later, though. She phoned Gladys. The houseboy, Ali, said very politely that Gladys was out. As always, she hated his near-BBC English, remembering his black face and fez.

Then she phoned Celia. Sidney, her husband, replied. Celia was in town. 'Are *you all right*, Margaret?' She said that she was and put the phone down quickly. He must have heard the gin.

She poured more gin, by accident the largest yet. This would stop her shaking. She went to the verandah.

There, over the inching shadows, the darting birds, the mellowing sky, that horrible image returned and imposed itself. Alec, with his bonny smile, wrinkles turned to dimples, was pressing down on a young black body, entwined in black limbs. She knew it hadn't happened. He would never . . .

But she knew it had, because it was more of an event in the world than those last awkward marital couplings nearly twenty years ago, before she and Alec had settled for separate bedrooms. The event had occurred in her head. It was occurring and would occur there over and over again. Wrestling bodies. Quiet laughter.

She herself laughed aloud bitterly. She must be going mad. She blinked at the jacaranda and thought of Spain. Gladys said there was bougainvillaea in Spain. Margaret wondered if there would be jacaranda.

When Agnes came back she would smile hard and say 'Thank you very much, Agnes' and ask about her school. Joseph must have returned. He could give Agnes food in the kitchen. She would thank Agnes and show her hospitality. Then it would be over. Africa would be over.

Egg Spells | Denny Simpson

Lizzie's dislocated eyeballs rested in the palm of his hand. They were the consistency of two softly boiled eggs. Maximilian carefully scrutinised each of the eyes, before dropping them gently on to the silver tray by his elbow. They looked so bald without their lashes.

She had been fifteen when he had met her on the Gower sands two years previously. He had watched her chase the wind into the sea and discover the corpse of the dog on the tide. Its pelt had been reduced to a hideous waxiness and the black pits of its eye sockets had been filled with pebbles. He had stepped in after her and cupped his hands against her face. That had been the first time he had felt her eyelashes brush against his fingers. Later, Lizzie Morgan told him that she lived on the beaches that fringed his estate. She ate raw birds' eggs, plucked from nests hidden in the salt-dry rushes of the shoreline. The day they found the dog, dried egg yolk had lain, like a crust of frost, across her right cheek. The sight of her stained face had prompted Maximilian to ask her to marry him. His tenants had been shocked. They knew Lizzie Morgan to be as daft as a spoon, but then there was no fool like an old fool. Maximilian knew he was old, particularly when he tried to run and keep up with a hanged man's daughter.

But once he started running after her, he could not stop. He could not stop now. Maximilian shifted Lizzie's new glass eyes between his curled fingers. They clicked together as he spun them around, faster and faster.

– I could knock the eyes out of your bastard head! So I could.

– Sorry, sorry, sorry.

– Everybody's always sorry, but it's always too late. Poor dog. But I'm hungry now. Will you buy me food, sir?

– Everything you could ever want, Lizzie.

– Will I wear a white dress in church?

– If you like. Do you love me, Lizzie Morgan?

– I loved my father. That's allowed. But you? I don't know.

Lizzie had never known very much about anything, unless she could bite into it and taste it, raw and unscented. She chewed up meals and titbits like a hungry wolf. Her teeth were slightly yellow and very crooked, but they were strong. Maximilian had screamed when she had bitten into his thigh and drawn blood as they made love for the first time in his tapestry-covered bed. It was the night after the day they had found the dog on the beach and he had proposed to her, as she stood sheltering behind his hands. Lizzie's teeth had carved into his body. She quite literally seemed to feed on him. Her incredible appetites – revealed both inside and outside the tapestried sanctity of the four-poster bed – revolted and shocked the household servants, but Maximilian de St Blaize adored his Lizzie.

He refused to alter a stitch of her dress, or improve a single one of her unpredictable manners. The neighbouring gentry avoided his company, but Lizzie seemed oblivious of their contempt towards her. She stretched herself out on the long dining table in the hall of her new home and chewed away at the strips of beef which her husband wrapped around his hands to feed her. He teased and tormented her, like he did one of his hunting hawks, hiding the food she desired until she appeared tamed and yielding, fresh for his plunder. Lizzie boasted the russet and cream colouring of a prize pheasant and she was as plump as a quail.

Like a bird, her instinct was to run for cover whenever strangers appeared, but she had faced Maximilian down when he had stood before her on the shoreline and asked her name. Unconcerned by his crushed-velvet-and-lace elegance, she had wiped away the egg yolk dribbling from the corners of her mouth and smiled up at him. Maximilian had seen a vision. His heart had pounded into a strange kind of fury. He would snatch up this strange jewel from the sands and run away with her to prevent another sharing in her dirty glory.

– *Lizzie Morgan, sir. That's my name, see. Baptised over there in the church with the green slate roof. And there was a special cake made me. But I couldn't eats then, I couldn't.*

– *You have been eating eggs, recently, I think.*

> – *I eats them here. I'm all day running, see.*
> – *I do see, Lizzie Morgan.*

He saw nothing but Lizzie Morgan. He pinned her against him, like a watch chain, and refused to acknowledge the outrage of his friends. After the outbreak of the war against Napoleon, husband and wife had gone to market to oversee the sale of Maximilian's prize sheep. He had marvelled at her lack of self-consciousness. She straddled the bars of the pens in the auction rooms, revealing legs bare of any covering except her own golden hair. In the tavern, she tore at her meat and potatoes with her hands, before stopping to clean them against the folds of her old print frock.

In the autumn following their marriage, she discovered an extraordinary emporium that had opened in the high street of the nearby market town.

> – *There is people from all over the country come to look in at its windows. They is painted gold and scarlet. And inside you can see strange creatures, like the ones sewn on the bed curtains. A Noah's Ark of a shop, to be sure.*

Lizzie handed him a pamphlet she had found on the street outside the shop and he read its contents out to her:

> 'The knowledge of my secrets I have gathered in my travels abroad (where I have spent my time ever since I was fifteen years old to this, my nine and twentieth year)

in France and Italy and in the Dark Continents. *Those that have travelled to these places might tell you what a miracle of art I have achieved to assist Nature in the preservation of her own Great works. In my shop, bear witness to the following marvels: two Elephants' heads can be seen attached to giant wooden shields. From each of their Ivory tusks swings a Monkey; below their bald feet, two Leopards paw the ground, Pythons coiled, like a lady's stole, around their necks. Two giant Turtles do walk at the heels of these rare beasts, each one ridden by three white Owls. These are the sights I promise you, I, Silas Trotter, gentleman and trader in Exotic Species, to be found at the house with the black dore, between the Sign of the Rose and Crown and Jacob's Well. Therefore be not unwilling to come, but suspend your Judgement till you have try'd and then speak as you find.'*

   – *Can I have a leopard?*
     – *Why a leopard?*
     – *It looks like it runs as fast as me.*

Lizzie Morgan's hands were as quick and agile as her running legs. She could steal eggs from under a mother hen's beak and she could spin yarn as fine as the floating seeds of a clock flower. Her hands traced Maximilian's tired old body like two jittery lacewings. She was a warm, living clod of a body, curled into his shoulder at night under the family's dusty heraldic trappings. Chilled by draughts and doubts, Maximilian fed on her blood-red heat. He felt his old heart tick with anticipation as she breathed against him. Strong, regular breaths. When Lizzie had died, the palms of her hands had turned up, as if in resignation at what lay before her. She died from an ugly tumour that had grown in her left breast. Her last breaths had been ugly and hoarse. Maximilian had plugged his ears with animal fat so that he could not hear her die, but her upturned palms had told their own story. They had flipped over like spun coins and the deed was done. Lizzie had been just seventeen the day she died.

Maximilian mourned his wife like one possessed. The six cooks employed in the kitchens were instructed to bake her favourite foods. They were then set out on big silver serving dishes to form a culinary garland around her black marble bier in the great hall. Meanwhile, Maximilian wandered through the fifty rooms of his house, catching glimpses of his wife's discarded clothing. He thought momentarily she must have come in from the sea and thrown off her clothes to dry out by one of the many fires they kept burning throughout the day. But then he remembered Lizzie's cold body lying in state on the dining table in the great hall. Maximilian had also grown very cold since his wife had died. He couldn't stay warm, even when sitting in the hall's inglenook fireplaces. No heat could warm him as Lizzie's hands and breath had done, and he missed her. Her empty skirts and bodices were all he had to fill out the hollow of his new life. He shook out the folds of her dresses and breathed up their eggy perfumed smell. Inside one he discovered the pamphlet advertising Trotter's Emporium for Exotic Species. The seeds of a new obsession were sown as once again he read his way through Silas Trotter's manifesto. Here was a man who, like the Bible's Noah, preferred to work in twos. Maximilian, deprived of his other half, found himself drawn by curiosity to visit the shop's premises.

He discovered Silas Trotter inside his emporium, an alligator slung across his shoulder like a flitch of bacon. This unexpected sight threw Maximilian off his guard initially, but after asking a few questions on the origins of such a wonderful-looking beast, he was soon lighting up his clay pipe and talking of distant shores with the shop owner. Silas could see from the cut of Maximilian's suit that he was a rich man, but he was also a much-troubled man. The pouches under his bloodshot eyes were grey and heavy with tiredness. His mouth rarely smiled, even at some of Silas's more outrageous anecdotes. He felt the unexpected encounter might lead to some profit for himself, however, so, leaning the alligator up against the shop wall, he pulled out an old armchair for his esteemed visitor to sit on. Maximilian was wearing a black velvet coat and his armband of mourning had not immediately been visible.

– A recent bereavement, sir?

– Just a day since my wife, my dear wife, passed away ...

Maximilian felt the tears start in his eyes. He hurried up from the armchair in order to avoid the other man's intense gaze. There was no escaping the fact that the taxidermist's eyes were as hard and unyielding as those of his stuffed animals. Maximilian felt uncomfortable, but not because of the reference to his armband. There was something else that worried him about the crowded, fusty interior of Trotter's Emporium for Exotic Species. It was the sense of being surrounded by dead flesh that nevertheless seemed to have a life of its own. Wherever he turned his attention, Maximilian found himself face to face with eyes that glinted in the half-lit shop interior, like dozens of tiny ebony beads. Hanging from the ceiling's wooden beams, like bunches of dried herbs, were a large quantity of horseshoe bats. Below their caped wings, foxes and stoats prowled across the floorboards, whilst the two alligators, lined up against the wall by Maximilian's elbow, seemed to be deep in a private conversation of their own devising. He felt a draught blow suddenly through the room and it was as if all the animals had together taken a sharp intake of breath and exhaled in harmony in memory of the deceased woman.

– A shame, sir. A great shame. My condolences. My heartfelt condolences. I, too, lost my wife to a terrible fever, just two years ago. There was nothing to be done, nothing.

Hearing this, Maximilian swung round on his toes and interrupted his host.

– Nothing, sir? Death is a foe, like one of your foxes here when he chased a farmer's hens. Nothing more, nothing less. He must be challenged and not ignored. That has been my mistake. And your mistake. We should seek to reverse that error of judgement.

– I applaud your courage. But what can be done?

– All of these creatures here once lived and breathed. Yes? Then you took their dead bodies and you restored them. They have not been left to rot in a grave, to lose all that once made them alive in the eyes of the world around them.

Silas had an acute sense of smell, vital if he were to check for any unfortunate leakages in his sales goods, but this time he smelled something different – *something out of the ordinary run of things*. He had not, of course, built up his extraordinary operation by being forward in going backwards. Silas had never known what it was to stand in a shadow. He ached for a spotlight and he invariably found one. He was a showman and a conjuror. *Now you see it, now you don't, ladies and gentlemen.* Death treading his remorseless path, but then sidetracked with a flick of a scalpel, wielded with the accuracy of a duellist. Or the cluster of brain cells teased out of the nostril with a hooked taper that might put you in mind of Casanova toying with an oyster – if you were ever lucky enough to experience such a sight. Sitting between the conversational alligators, Maximilian learnt more about a deed that he had only wildly grasped at when reading Silas's pamphlet. Lizzie could be returned to him in all her russet and cream glory. She need never decay into a pile of brittle bones inside the charnel house that sat under a plinth of outstanding banality constructed by his late – unmourned – uncle. Silas could preserve her with the potions and needles of his trade. He need only provide the fee.

– It is possible then, sir, to preserve human flesh and not just that of an animal?

Maximilian took another look around the shop and encountered the watchful ebony eyes of the foxes, stoats and alligators parading its floorboards. How well they simulated Nature, even in the frozen poses of death. The fox standing by his right foot looked as if it could take flight the moment a pack of hounds were scented at his brushy tail. Beside the fox was a stoat which lurched upwards on hind legs, a bamboo frame large enough to take the weight of a gentleman's top hat clasped between its front paws. Maximilian mopped his brow with his pocket handkerchief and pondered the complex mysteries of Silas's unusual trade. If all that lives must die, what of these strange animals that faked a life? Their resurrection was aided and abetted by phials of foul-smelling amber liquids, which were hoarded on narrow shelves running across the back wall of the shop. Maximilian assumed the strange odour carried throughout the room emanated from these jars and bottles, but he was not sure. Lizzie had died in the stench of her own rotting body which had smelt as rank as these unnamed liquids. Maximilian inhaled again and registered the sharp tang of yet another strange, spicy chemical.

– If you were to carry out such an operation, sir, I must ask of you one favour.

– Name it.

Silas now scented the whiff of victory, over and above the acrid stink of the oil he had used to clean down the alligators' skins. His usually impenetrable exterior – as tough to gauge as the tautened skin of a dead alligator – underwent a sudden transformation. A smile broke out over the latticework of wrinkles covering his hollowed cheeks and Maximilian, still in awe of the many-clawed spectators around him, visibly started on catching sight of the taxidermist's very white, very real-looking teeth so close to his own living eyes. Silas explained that he had had them filed down from fragments of a broken porcelain basin. He whipped them out of his mouth and brandished them in front of Maximilian's shocked face, before popping them back in so he could begin his next speech.

– What you see, dear sir, is not always what you expect. A lesson in life's mysteries, I think. But your request?

– That I attend the operation throughout. Please.

Silas chewed on his porcelain teeth for some minutes whilst he absorbed this plea. No other client had ever asked to attend an embalming before and he was temporarily at a loss for words. Certain aspects of his profession were of necessity shrouded in secrecy. He was a hunter, a smuggler, a man who contravened the very basic laws of Nature, let alone the tenets of Christianity. He brought back the dead and he traded their corpses for profit. *A stitch in time and a fortune is mine* was this man's motto. Silas Trotter was a name that a small band of cognoscenti recognised and admired, but many others flinched with horror when they heard he was loose in their midst. Luckily, the widower Maximilian had only one point of reference: his dead Lizzie. He thought of her now, lying unattended amongst dozens of plates of uneaten delicacies, and wept loudly, unrestrained by the presence of the stranger seated beside him.

– I beg you, sir. Meet my request. What cause would I have to interrupt your work? Or to broach its mysteries beyond my own circle?

Silas watched Maximilian's tears fall on to his shaking hands and relented. He was not moved by pity, or even by profit, on this occasion. What he sensed was a rare opportunity to test his skills. Maximilian's desire that he pickle a human body to outlast the centuries would ensure that his name would survive alongside that of the preserved corpse. He had had all too few opportunities to work on human flesh in the past.

– What a tribute to the lady's beauty, dear sir. That you intend creating a portrait unlike any other to remember her by. I salute such appreciation of my art, as well, of course, as evidence of your great passion and devotion.

– Your own wife, sir?

– She is with me still.

Silas leered and tapped at his set of porcelain teeth.

– It was her sink, dear sir, which I smashed to pieces. I am not one to show emotion as a rule, but I was driven to distraction when she made a bad deal over some tigers I had spent several years trying to obtain for a very particular gentleman. *Marjory Postlethwaite, you are a damned fool*, I cried. *You, sir*, she replied, *will eat my words one day*. Which I suppose I do whenever I have occasion to quote her, God rest her soul. She was not, you understand, much in the way of a businesswoman.

Silas shook his head and then Maximilian shook his hand. It was long and lean with five beautifully manicured nails, each with a neat white half-moon. They were not what he expected from a man who dealt with jars of obnoxious poisons. Maximilian shuddered, stepped back and stumbled over the hat-bearing stoat.

– You will come to my house this evening, sir. There can be no delay.

Saying this, Maximilian gathered up his hat, gloves and stick and exited Trotter's Emporium for Exotic Species. His brain stung with what he had heard, seen and inhaled during the past four hours. Yes. Four hours had passed since he had stepped through Trotter's doorway. He checked his pocket watch and read its dial with a sense of shock. It seemed that his initial terror at Lizzie's abandonment of him had been transformed into a rare kind of courage with this encounter. He had succeeded in making a bargain with a man who tinkered with life and death as if they were no more than a pair of dodgy cogs in the workings of a rundown carriage clock. Could it really be that simple to reverse the accepted order of things?

Maximilian de St Blaize came from a long line of baronets, bishops and admirals. He owed his blue blood to an eclectic inbreeding of no more than half a dozen families at most, all drawn from the ranks of minor European royals and the local aristocracy. He went to church on Sunday because he had always gone to church on Sunday. He ate beef because he had always eaten beef. He wore dubbined boots of leather and took snuff because that was the custom. He became a magistrate and then a Member of Parliament for a very rotten borough because that was expected of him. He let men hang – and once a pregnant girl – because the law said that was what should happen if sheep got stolen, or a shawl was whisked away from a shop counter without paying. It was the nature of things. Time had passed and Maximilian had put his rather wonderful wax seal to a succession of bills from gentlemen outfitters, the estate accounts, invitations to dine and orders of execution. And then he had seen a girl with an egg-smeared face, her hands full of broken shells, and his world had been shaken to its very static roots. He had married Lizzie Morgan after hanging her father. He had married an illiterate girl from a family which owned only its name; worse, he had married for love. His mother had fainted on hearing the news and had promptly removed herself to Leamington Spa to take a water cure. Meanwhile, her only son and the estate's heir had finally discovered happiness at the grand old age of fifty-nine and he had enjoyed every minute of it. Reflecting on these things, Maximilian began to feel less afraid of Silas Trotter and his potions. His life had done a cartwheel once before and all had not been lost. He could spin it over again and he would survive and this time his lovely Lizzie would stay with him. Maximilian put away his watch and beckoned to his coachman, whom he had ordered to wait for him in a discreet backstreet.

– We must hurry, Jude. I have a special visitor coming and there are preparations to be made.

Jude whipped up the horses, but Silas still managed to reach the mansion in advance of his host, complete with two very large leather holdalls. They rattled loudly as they were hauled up the entrance steps and into the library where Silas was installed to begin work on his unique portrait of a dead lady. The stranger issued his instructions and the baronet obeyed, much to the incredulity of his servants. Maximilian had the long deal table brought up from the kitchen, along with a number of big basins and trays. After several hours of furniture shifting and candle lighting, the library door was closed on the two men and a deep silence reigned within for the next twenty-four hours.

What thoughts came into Maximilian's mind as Silas made the first incision into his wife's naked body? The first cut ran from her sternum to the bottom of her navel. She opened up like a soft leather purse for the embalmer's long yellow fingers, which turned and twisted inside her folds of muscle and tissue. Maximilian stood by Silas's side throughout the operation, mesmerised at the revelation of his wife's inner workings. He felt the same degree of absorption as when a horologist flipped open the back of his watch to repair its faulty gearing system. This was the essence of his dear Lizzie? A pile of wet intestines? The stubby pulp of a heart severed from its fleshy home? He felt fascinated by the intricate webs of nerve and sinew he saw stretched out before him. Not even the sound of Silas's careful stitching, drawing together the loose flaps of his wife's skin, shocked him.

Silas was unquestionably a craftsman of the highest order. He worked with great grace, looping cat gut thread into his needle and then knotting up its ends beneath the folds of Lizzie's white skin. Her diseased breast had been removed and replaced with a leather counterfeit stuffed with straw, before he began plying his needle in a series of herringbone stitches which worked their way up her unbreathing chest, like an eel gliding through water. Finally, her hollow eye sockets were filled with the glass replicas that Maximilian had carried around the house with him in the quiet hours of early morning. A pair of blue eyes. As blue as the thrush eggs Lizzie had once gorged on the shoreline.

– They looked so bald without eyelashes, but now . . .

– You will retire, sir, whilst I add the finishing touches, Silas said gently.

He could see that Maximilian was overwhelmed at the sight of his new glass-eyed Lizzie. She did indeed look a little fresher, although the air in the library stank of the evidence of her unnatural preservation order. Silas had dressed her in the white frock she had worn in church for her wedding. It was as loose and fine as the membrane of an egg. Then he had painted her face in a light coating of cosmetics. A touch of powder and rouge and some cochineal paste for her lips.

– Now, lady, you are ready, Silas whispered into her cold ear.

He folded her hands across her breasts with great delicacy, as if trying to prevent her from waking, and then blew out the candles that stood too close to the body. In the softer light, Lizzie Morgan did indeed look as if she had just fallen asleep. Silas smiled. His genius was reflected in her glass eyes, which, thanks to the subdued lighting, had lost their shiny, manufactured surface. He stepped over to the door and called out to the baronet. Then he withdrew into the corridor as Maximilian stood hesitantly in the doorway. It was only a short distance to the kitchen table, but those few yards worked a most miraculous effect, easing out the more obvious signs of Lizzie's true state. He shuffled forwards, almost afraid to look upon her, so beautiful, so peaceful, so close to his touch, but not too close. He paused by her feet, which were still bare, and marvelled at what he finally allowed himself to see: Lizzie's cheeks glowed again, like they had on the shoreline. Her eggshell-blue eyes reflected the lights around her and they seemed as alive as they had ever been. Maximilian reached into his coat pocket and drew out a small bird's egg. Picking up one of the empty bowls beside the table, he cracked it open, careful to keep its yolk unbroken. Then he dipped his fingers into the egg and tenderly stroked them down the side of his wife's face.

– And there was a special cake made you. But you couldn't eats then, could you? But you have been eating eggs, recently, I think, Lizzie Morgan?

Maximilian was to ask her this same question every night for the next twelve years. That was how long Lizzie Morgan stayed with him after her resurrection, comfortably arranged on a sedan bed situated at the end of the old four-poster.

– *Oh, yes, I eats them here. I'm all day running, see.*

Always the same words from the hard painted lips he felt under his yolk-stained fingers.

I do see, Lizzie Morgan, I do see was Maximilian's own unchanging reply.

Quality of Life | Amanda Coe

He had had lots of dreams about UFOs lately. Except they were buses, double-deckers like the ones he took most days, red and unremarkable but for the fact that once he had bought his ticket from the driver and found a seat it struck him that he was actually sitting on a UFO. Ray wasn't frightened by this, but so excited and full of expectation that he woke up anyway. Awake, the dream quickly congealed into absurdity. But it was always a dream he was happy to reinhabit, one of those small bits of luck that made you glad, like getting the pretty girl to serve you in the newsagent.

Sometimes he was sitting on the UFO and it was Louise who woke him. He and Louise had been married for forty-two years, and his nights with her had always been interrupted because she was a snorer. There was no stopping her knotted, plosive arias once they were underway, and she often dropped off first. She was a good couple of stone heavier than him, and it was a job to shift her from her back on to her side, so Ray learned to bear with it until the noise reached its crescendo and, with a monstrous, amplified hog bellow, Louise finally woke even herself up. 'Sorry love,' she'd whisper humbly, and then turn over, docile and silent.

That was before she began to die. Now the sounds she brought to the night were arhythmic and unpredictable. Moans, sporadic, gentle, like surface bubbles that relieved the lava pressure of the pain seething beneath. On bad nights, these joined together, boiling into a scream that almost made her pain into his. 'Please God make it stop,' she begged, over and over again. There was nothing he could do. Kneeling on all fours seemed to bring her some relief, panting as though she was in labour. He rubbed her back, said, 'There you are old girl,' over and over again. It could be hours. Sometimes the pain stopped quite suddenly. Sometimes it didn't stop at all, and the morning began. He made her hot-water bottles, brought her her pills, increasingly a little bit early. She was waiting for the next dose almost as soon as she'd taken them. It was best when she got a few hours of sleep in between.

The doctor had explained to Louise that there was a problem with calcium levels in her blood, which they were trying to sort out with the various drugs she was on. The doctor had explained to Ray that the calcium in Louise's bloodstream was being released from her spine as cancer ate into it. They agreed that hearing this wouldn't be any help to her at all.

Since Louise didn't officially know that she was dying, she and Ray didn't talk about it. They talked a lot about Christmas, which for the first time ever was not to be spent at home, but with their son, Patrick, who lived near Newcastle. He had promised them Christmas dinner at a hotel, and Louise fretted over what to wear, She had one outfit she thought was smart enough to pass, a suit which she'd worn to her niece's wedding six years before. But when she put it on she looked like a little girl playing with her mother's clothes; even her shoes were too big.

'I don't want to show our Patrick up,' she said anxiously. Ray told her not to worry, they'd get her something else. She felt too bad to go into town with him but he asked her about colours and sizes and went off to the shop she told him. He'd never bought her anything to wear before. He felt embarrassed, but the manageress was nice enough when he'd explained the situation to her. She was what Ray considered a handsome woman, tall, with rigidly sprayed hair in a colour that didn't match her eyebrows. Good legs. Louise's legs had been what first got him talking to her. They'd gone to little stalks now.

The manageress picked out a dress with a sort of long waistcoat but it was over eighty pounds. 'Out of our league I'm afraid love,' Ray told her. The woman didn't seem to mind. She found another dress instead, blue. That was over forty pounds but he wasn't going to say no again after she'd taken so much time with him. When he handed over the notes to pay for it, it crossed his mind that it was a lot of money wasted if Louise didn't live long enough to wear the thing.

'Can I bring it back, if it's not right?' he asked. The manageress said of course, they would exchange it for something his wife preferred. Ray left it at that.

Louise didn't try the dress on when he brought it back, although she nodded and smiled at it and said it was lovely. He could tell she was bad. She hadn't even picked up her knitting. She'd always had phases of knitting things: toys and baby clothes and jumpers. It used to drive him up the wall sometimes, the tic of her needles like tiny teeth snapping when he was trying to watch the snooker or the cricket. Now she didn't stop. It was dolls she knitted mostly, soldiers and policemen and milkmaids and clowns and ballerinas with elaborate costumes and the same smiling face, button-eyed, with rosy cheeks made from a licked red drawing pencil. She gave the dolls to church bazaars, to the children of relatives and friends and neighbours, to Ray to raffle off for the Normandy Veterans, and their living-room was still crammed with the surplus. Once upon a time he wouldn't have stood them there, attracting dust. But he'd got used to them now, they were company, and the bright colours cheered him up.

'You fancy a cup of tea, Dad?' Louise said to him. It used to mean that she was going to make one for him; now it was the opposite. She lived on tea, couldn't keep much else down, apart from the odd banana and a bit of toast now and again. He went into the kitchen to put the kettle on. There was a darning needle out on the table. He hadn't left it there.

'What's this needle doing here, Louise?'

'What needle?'

He brought the needle in to show her. You could see the time it took for things to travel from her eyes to her brain. She smiled, dimples.

'I've been feeding the Christmas cake.'

'It can't take much more, can it?'

'I know what I'm doing, you leave it alone.'

He went back into the kitchen and opened the pantry door. The lid of the old Jacob's biscuit tin gave a buckled chord as he lifted it. She'd fed it all right. The brandy fumes came off the cake, moist with fruit. Louise had made the cake back in October, like she always did, a few weeks after the pickling was over. She was vain about her Christmas cakes. She used to make ten or more, for giving to family and friends. Anyone who got one was solicited for praise at each visit, regardless of previous assurances that the cake had been delicious. This could go on as late as Easter.

Ray and Patrick used to wind her up, when Patrick lived at home. A few days after Christmas, when their cake had already been quarried into several times, and they were sitting round having a slice with their cup of tea, Patrick would start.

'Not sure about this cake, Mrs V,' he'd say.

Louise rose to it immediately. 'What's up with it?' she'd protest. 'It's all right in't it, Dad?'

'Bit dry,' Ray might chip in, or, 'Bit too clarty.'

Her eyes would flick between the two of them, wary yet delighted. They were careful not to look at each other.

'I don't know about you, but I like a bit more marzipan as well,' one of them would go on to remark, saying 'marzipan' to get her goat, because it was a point of pride that she made her own almond paste to put on it, with nothing artificial, instead of using bought marzipan like other people did. Then she'd smile, knowing they didn't mean it. It was the same every year except the one when she'd had the oven turned down too low and the cake came out not properly cooked in the middle. Ray and Patrick ate it without comment. Tormented by their silence, Louise finally asked them if it was all right.

'Delicious, Louise,' Ray said.

'Very nice,' added Patrick, closing the subject.

This year there was just the one cake, to take to Patrick's. Louise iced it a week before Christmas. Ray offered to help, but Louise told him to stay out of the kitchen. It took her nearly all evening. Ray nodded off in his chair while he was waiting for *The X-Files* to start and managed to get a few hours' sleep. Louise called him in when the cake was finished, waking him. Looking at it, you couldn't have told there was a thing wrong with her. The sides were covered with firmly forked peaks and the top was bounded with soft little pillows of icing, each cushioning a silver ball. There was a robin on a log in one corner, a plastic snowman in another, a tiny brush-bristle fir tree in the third corner, and in the fourth, a kicking football player in Everton blue.

'Not very Christmassy, that, Louise,' Ray said about the football player.

'I found it in me box. It was from one of our Patrick's birthday cakes.'

The night before Christmas Eve, Ray wound up his watch and set both alarm clocks by the time check on the radio. Patrick was driving over in the morning to take them back to his house, and though he'd never been an early riser they were both worried that they might oversleep. Everything was ready; the cake in its tin, some bought mince pies and sausage rolls, although Patrick had said not to bother, Patrick's present wrapped up – a pair of driving gloves. Their bags and sponge bags were packed.

In fact, Louise had a bad night with the excitement, and neither of them slept a wink. Towards five, as she lowed with pain, Ray got up to make her a hot-water bottle. It was cold in the kitchen. As he waited for the kettle to boil, Ray broke off one of the little icing cushions from the top of Louise's cake and popped it in his mouth. Its sweetness vanished almost before he could taste it, hard, then liquid, then gone. There was just the silver ball left. He rolled it around his mouth with his tongue and looked out of the window. Humming silence pressed round the house. It was at these times that Ray most dearly hoped that he might see something in the rectangle of sky above the school playing fields. A shape, hovering. Despite his belief that extraterrestrial life forms were continually trying to communicate, he'd never had a sighting. There was just the sky, lifting into dawn, a satellite blinking. But he had hopes for where Patrick lived, on the moors outside Newcastle. There had been a cluster of sightings at a spot just a couple of miles away from Patrick's village. It would be no hardship for Patrick to drive him out there, and of course Louise didn't have to come.

She was a miracle on Christmas Day. The new dress made her eyes more blue than grey and for the first time in months she was behind them all day, the old Louise. She'd had the hairdresser to the house that week, so she looked a picture, except that Ray couldn't get used to her being so small. He got Patrick to take a photograph of them both, standing in his living-room just before they went out to the hotel.

Amanda Coe

'In't it lovely?' Louise kept saying, as they walked into the hotel lobby, as they had a drink in the bar before their dinner, when the prawn cocktail came and then the turkey and the pudding. She picked at the food and then surprised them both by polishing off the whole plate of Christmas pudding and custard. She'd always had a sweet tooth.

'You've done us proud, son,' Ray told Patrick, as the waitress brought coffee and chocolate mints. A pretty girl with bad ankles. Louise sat bolt upright in her chair, taking in all the families around them, dimpling the minute anyone caught her eye. As Ray saw her smile at the waitress he suddenly imagined himself on his knees in front of their Patrick, who was built like a house side, violently burrowing his head into the spongy comfort of his paunch.

'I think your mother's getting tired,' he said. Louise was indignant. 'I'm not tired,' she insisted, 'I'm brilliant.' But they both told her it was time they were making a move.

After Louise had gone off to bed, Ray and Patrick drank beer in front of the TV and talked about cricket. The year before, Patrick had paid for his parents to have a satellite dish installed so that Ray could keep up with it, and the football. He'd been a good lad to them. He'd lived at home until he was twenty-seven, but since he'd moved away he'd helped them out a lot. New three-piece suite, the satellite dish, a fridge freezer. He was doing well at his job, sent all over the country as a rep. Louise boasted about him to everyone she met. Her dearest wish was to see him married and settled, but she knew it wasn't going to happen. Patrick had a lady friend, but she was a divorcée

208

with a couple of kids Patrick couldn't stand. Spoiled rotten, he said.

'Fancy a bit of cake?' asked Patrick. Since Louise wasn't there to object, they put their slices of pork pie on the same plate as the cake, to save washing-up.

They ate in silence. The cake was up to Louise's usual standard. 'Well, if that's Christmas we've had it,' said Ray finally, as he trapped the last stray sultana with his forefinger and transferred it to his mouth.

That night he had the UFO dream again. He was on the bus, and this time the inspector got on at the next stop, except he was the chief extraterrestrial. Instead of asking for Ray's ticket, when he got to him he said, 'What do you want to know?' Ray was impressed by the importance of this but unable to answer. The inspector stood there, waiting. Ray offered his ticket. Everyone on the bus was staring at him; he felt himself heating with incipient shame. 'What do you want to know?' the inspector repeated, peremptory and impatient. Ray woke up. He thought it was a very fair point. If you made contact, you had to be prepared, it could last only a matter of seconds. But he couldn't think of a good question.

The Boxing Day weather was raw and Ray tried to get Louise to stay at home, but she said she'd enjoy the drive. There wasn't much to see in the way of countryside because the windows were fogged with the heating and in any case a sleety pall cut off views after about fifty yards. Ray knew that conditions were far from perfect for a sighting but he couldn't help hoping.

It was the top of a rigg, they called it round there, no village or anything for miles. If there'd been a bit of sun the view would probably have been worth taking in. Louise stayed in the car with the engine running to keep the heat up. Patrick lumbered after Ray, although Ray would rather have been alone. There was a footpath up to the top. It made a shambles of his shoes, all mud. Patrick was more out of breath than him when they stopped, with his bulk. They stood for a while, not speaking. There was the roar from the motorway in the background, otherwise you might think it was the end of the world. Patrick coughed.

'You're not having much luck old son,' he said. He rubbed his hands together against the cold. With his sheepskin coat he put Ray in mind of a football manager watching from the dugout.

'Points of light moving in formation, that's what they've seen,' Ray told him. 'First sighting August 1963 and eleven sightings since then, the last just over a year ago. All the descriptions tally.'

'Well there's bugger all today, I'll tell you.'

Ray didn't want to go back yet. 'Damn,' he said. 'I meant to bring the ruddy camera.'

'What are you going to take a picture of, nowt?' said Patrick, but he still offered to go back to the car for it. When he'd gone, Ray stared hard into the sky. He'd always imagined himself alone at the moment of contact. Maybe there was something, a sort of tingling coming up from the ground, but it could have been vibrations from traffic on the motorway. Ray tried again to think of a question, but all he came up with was daft lines

from science fiction films like 'What do you want from us?' and
'Do you come in peace?' Patrick returned with the camera. Ray
aimed it at the blank sky and took two shots, one facing north,
one south. He made a precise note of the time, just in case. One
thirty-two, one thirty-three.

'We'll have to get a move on before the pub stops doing
food,' Patrick said. Louise had fallen asleep in the car.

It was her last really good day. Only a couple of nights after
they got back home Ray woke to find her pulling underclothes
out of the dressing-table drawers, her best handbag crooked in
her right arm. She said that she was looking for her mother's
jewellery. Her mother hadn't left her any jewellery apart from
a garnet ring that she always wore. He showed her it, on the
bedside table with her watch. Her eyes were gone, sliding all
over the place. She started batting him with her handbag.

'You keep off me, I know you're trying to take my money!'
she shouted.

The metal clasp caught him above his right eye. Furious tears
scorched his throat. He almost hit her back.

'You're mad, woman,' Ray shouted at her. He left her to it.
When he came back from making a cup of tea she was asleep
on the bed, her handbag and her mouth both open, like fish
that had died stranded.

The doctor said that the calcium had started to affect Louise's
brain. Either that, or the painkillers were making her see things;
he didn't make himself clear. Even a week after Christmas, Ray
couldn't believe that she'd been fit to go out to a hotel and be
seen in company. It was her shouting with pain, or shouting at

him that he'd had other women or was taking her money or had got her pregnant. When she'd just had her drugs he could look forward to a couple of hours of tranced silence, but otherwise she ran him ragged. The nurse who had been coming once a week doubled her visits, giving him a couple of mornings off to go into town and do their shopping. He often came back without things, even if he made a list. He walked around with the film from Christmas in his coat pocket, meaning to take it in for developing when he was picking up Louise's prescription from the chemist, but he always got home before he remembered. These lapses worried him, as though Louise had infected him with her dementia.

The doctor talked to Ray about quality of life and pain management and Ray agreed that it would be best to put Louise in hospital. The consultant said there was nothing more they could do, except keep her comfortable. Ray knew she would be frightened, but she needed a drip to nourish her and to keep her fed with drugs. Patrick came down for the day, so that he could visit on the first night. She'd settled in by then, and was praising the nurses.

He hadn't been alone in the dark for forty-two years. Every night, Ray left the radio on, tuned to a local station that had a phone-in programme, up just enough so that voices murmured in the background. Otherwise it was too quiet to sleep. Sometimes the conversations or the news headlines threaded themselves into his dreams so that he got confused about where he'd heard things. He thought he might have liked the peace during the day, but he was waiting for visiting hours from the moment he woke up. He did a lot of housework, vacuuming and dusting daily. He made a special trip to Boots to get the Christmas film developed. He even fixed a handle on the sideboard that Patrick had broken when he was in primary school. Louise's dolls watched him all the time with their identical eyes. Ray wished he could put them away, but he didn't like to.

After Louise had been in hospital for eight days, the nurse told Ray she'd been up in the night, pulling out all her drips, shouting there were burglars and the nurse wasn't to worry, she'd get rid of them. Ray told her off about it, but Louise smiled at him wearily, not remembering. He took the wallet of photos out to show her. He'd picked them up on the way to the hospital. Louise didn't raise her hands to take the photos when he passed them to her, so he laid them out on the bedspread beneath her chin, like a hand of patience. Her body barely interrupted the plane of the covers.

The photos jumped from the summer, when he'd started the film, to Christmas. It shocked him how substantial Louise had looked back in August, posing by her laden rose bush. Then she shrank into her blue dress, the two of them standing stiffly in Patrick's living-room. Patrick at the hotel, with his arm around his mother, disappearing at the edge of the frame. The front of the hotel. Patrick's car parked in his drive, Patrick smirking uneasily with one hand on the bonnet. Two grey bits of sky. A shot he couldn't make out at first, like the camera had gone off by accident. It was skewed, and when he turned the photo round to a diamond shape Ray saw that it was him and Patrick, walking away from the camera on the footpath to the rigg.

You could just see the top of his head and Patrick's head and shoulders, framed asymmetrically in a dark mass that extended to the edges of the print. Above them in this frame was the same grey sky as in his photos, except for a tight oval of bluish light which saturated one corner of the image. Ray puzzled over the picture, organising its information into sense. The dark border suddenly resolved itself into the car window frame. Louise must have taken the photograph from inside the car, as he and Patrick walked to the top of the rigg. But the light. He showed the photo to Louise.

'You took this.' She nodded, smiling, the famous dimples. He jabbed at the light in the corner. 'What was that? Louise?'

His tone made her raise her head for a proper look. The other photos slithered to the sides of the bed. 'It's the sunshine.'

'There wasn't any sun that day. Don't you remember, woman?'

She'd faded off. He picked up the rest of the photos and put them back in the wallet. He looked again at her photo. It couldn't be the sun, even if the sun had been shining. And he knew that it hadn't been. Patrick would remember.

'Louise.'

Her eyes were shut.

'Louise, what did you take the picture for?' He shook her arm, made her open her eyes and look again. 'Why did you take the picture?'

'It's you and our Patrick.'

'I know who it bloody is. This light – what did you see?'

She swallowed thickly, a frown of pain shot through her features.

'Thirsty,' she said.

Notes and Queries | Phill Whitaker

It isn't true, what Mr Sudbury thinks. I *am* interested in things.

I'm interested in the crows by the side of the motorway; hard-men of the bird world, unconcerned by juggernauts rending the air just feet away. I'm also keen to learn exactly how it should be that ants have come to milk aphids. I wish to know what happens when a bullet, fired straight up in the sky, stops climbing. Does someone miles away get hurt as it falls to earth? And I'm fascinated by the impossibly fast chopping of a kitchen knife, how the chef keeps his fingers. Most chefs are perpetually halfway through a bottle of wine. My father was, anyway.

So, Mr Sudbury, I don't think anyone who really knows me would dispute the fact that I *am* interested in things. It's just that no one knows me. Not really. Excepting Edward, a bit. And Father, of course, though I'm trying not to let Father come into this.

Edward is my brother. Father was – it should go without saying – my father, though he has been other things besides. Mr Sudbury is . . . well, Mr Sudbury is a man who has only appeared in my life for nine minutes at any one time. And I doubt tomorrow will be any different.

Edward and I share this house, the same house in which we each did what growing up we were to do. Wine, beer; Bill lad, come here. Come and give your old man a kiss.

In some ways I regard it as my house, one in which Edward is fortunate to lodge. I, after all, am the one who has stuck it out here. Edward (in my mind) will forever be dogged by the Rita years. However, to those who know about wills and probate, the house is jointly ours, Edward's and mine.

And actually, we have come to an accommodation – two men, neither far off fifty. In fact, the only thing which irritates me about Edward is his recently acquired love of television soaps. And, I suppose, the fact that he occasionally brings up the subject of Father. The latter upset I deal with simply, by walking from the room, going upstairs without a single word.

Mr Sudbury first came into my life thirty-five years following my mother's departure from it. He was around half my age and had something called an MBA, according to his business card. I was forty-five. As he might put it himself, Mr Sudbury is quite a recent thing.

He had his advent around the time that passengers disappeared, to be replaced by customers.

'Sudbury,' he introduced himself, proffering a white envelope. 'That's the improvement grant. It's for you, to spend on local produce to . . .' he glanced around him, sniffing the February alr '. . . brighten this place up a bit. Hanging baskets, a fresh lick of paint, that sort of thing. The Works and Maintenance boys will be down next week with the new signs. See what you can do. Try and blend in with the corporate image.'

He stayed precisely nine minutes, arriving on the Nottingham-bound train, departing on that bound for London. There was nowhere for him to stay, even if he'd wanted to. The Station Hotel closed down twenty-four years ago.

Edward has worked all his life at the power station whose fat cooling towers belch continuously over our landscape. He drives a tipper truck. His day consists of numerous journeys from the huge stockpiles of coal, over to the hoppers which feed the furnaces. Goodness knows how many kilowatt hours he's had a hand in generating.

Even with everything which has gone on in recent years – pit closures, nuclear, gas – Edward is secure in his job. There has never been a sniff of redundancy. True, the coal now comes from Poland. But it appears (much to Edward's delight) that for the rest of his working life at least, there will always be the need for people to scoop that coal and drive it from one place to another.

I was born the year the war ended. That should have made me a symbol of hope. Mother left my life when I was ten. For months afterwards I wrote her letters and drew her pictures in my drawing book. She never came back. Father died when I was twenty-four, when Edward was twenty-one. Wine, beer;

Bill lad, come here. Come and give your old man a kiss. He never lived to see men walk on the moon.

When I was very young, much younger than ten anyway, I used to swing on the half-door of the ticket collector's booth at the station. The station master then was a fat man – one of the first Asian immigrants and a singular sight because of it. I used to hang on his gate, feet tucked off the ground, and put myself in his place. A station master. Donkey jacket and thick black trousers, complete with red stripe braiding the seams.

I used to imagine the pride which would transform my mother's face when I could finally usher her through that barrier. In my mind I would salute her, her dress billowing and the wisps of hair hanging delicately in front of the sticky-out ears she passed on to me. She would never need a ticket – her son ran the station. Her beloved son William Butler.

Memories of Mother (holding pegs for her as she hangs out clothes, showing her the hedgehog in the mint patch) are mostly of times when I managed to turn her mouth into a smile. Other things: Mother comforting me on her lap, when a pin hidden in a rug made its way into my bare foot, her skinny flesh transformed into both cushion and protective cage. Mother leaving me at the school gate on my first day – and being there, as promised, when the afternoon was done. Mother having Edward, feeding him from her breast; my never having her to myself again.

But also I remember my mother by the rows with Father, often late at night, when he'd get home from the hotel, drunk on wine and beer. Frequently, crockery would smash. Occasionally

I would hear the crack of hand on cheek; the dull noise a body makes as it hits a kitchen cupboard.

My eighth birthday. Unable to sleep, I slip into my parents' bedroom, sometime in the early hours, after I hear Father bang the front door. No row tonight. In the curtain-filtered gloom, I can make out her torso. The breast nearest me is flopped back with gravity, her nipple a dark smudge. Father's mouth closes over it. He groans. My mother is silent. Blankets slither over sheets. The air smells of stale beer. I leave as quietly as I can. My eighth birthday.

Tomorrow, Mr Sudbury comes. He will stay for nine minutes. Ever after, my life will be changed. The third time my life has never been the same again.

'A great chance, Butler,' he told me, hopping on to the London-bound train after his last visit, when he came to break the news. 'You married?'

'No.'

He nodded knowingly, though he could never understand. 'Well then, a great chance to develop some new interests.'

The only photograph that exists of my mother now stands on the mantelpiece. I found it in Father's top drawer, when the police finally let me clear his room. She stares a sepia stare. Her mouth is smiling. To me, her eyes look weary.

Father made food – master chef, flashing blade; in reality the cheapest cook the Station Hotel could find. On working days he made steak and kidney pies when travelling salesmen stayed, and drank in the bar when they didn't. Some nights, after the front door banged, he would come up to say goodnight. Wine, beer; Bill lad, come here. Come and give your old man a kiss. On days off, taking a break from the garden, he would sit with me on the step by the back door, shirt open over white vest, sleeves rolled up over hairy forearms, and tell me tales of spiders who ate their spouses, of ants who milked aphids, and of black spot which ravaged his roses.

An indecent two days after Father's funeral, Rita appeared.

He'd cut his wrists to shreds in the bath. We buried him in the municipal graveyard, faces down-turned with shame, while the neighbours' curtains quivered and a policeman stood at the door.

Rita was sat there with Edward, chewing cornflakes like cud, when I came down after another night mobile and awake.

'Bill, this here's Reet.'

Reet managed a brief smile before shovelling another spoonful into her mouth, much as I imagine Edward shovels coal.

Edward was twenty-one. Rita was his first girlfriend. The first inkling I had of her extreme youth came in the bathroom, where I happened across a bottle of something which professed itself capable of salvaging even the most acned complexion.

'Is she moving in?' I managed finally, catching him alone on the landing that evening.

'Reckon so.'

'She can't.'

Edward has never caught up the three years' start I had

on him. He didn't argue. I didn't ask, but I was told some weeks later that they were renting the flat above the barber's. Something for the weekend every day, if required.

Alone in a scandalised world, I would walk the two miles to the new motorway. As I trudged the hedge-lined lanes, I would think about spiders; whether they forgot the spouse they'd eaten, when the mating was done. And I thought about black spot, wondering what earthly reason it could have for ravaging roses. An hour at a time I would lean on the bridge railings, watching the traffic coursing below, and the contentedly strutting crows. They paid no heed to the lorries rending the air just feet away.

In those hours of contemplation, I came to see Edward's placid departure for what it was. The police – with awkward courtesy – had offered me accommodation away from the house, until they'd finished in the garden. I refused.

Shortly afterwards our family's story was wiped from the papers by the moon-landing. I stared at the dots of black and white, fuzzy pictures of a landmark in history. And I wondered why in such a world – no one travelled in underwear any more, why people no longer came to eat Father's steak and kidney pies, and stay in the Station Hotel.

Tomorrow, Mr Sudbury comes. I lie awake, furious that this should be happening to me. Memories of Father – master chef, flashing blade; in reality the cheapest cook the Station Hotel could find – refuse to be subdued.

Downstairs Edward is watching TV. I can hear the voices.

They're indistinct, but I know the programme's about a women's prison, somewhere in Australia. During the evening, he has feasted upon the dramas and joys of made-up people in streets and hospitals around the world.

Earlier on, I joined Edward to watch the news. Gunmen, in a country I will never visit, fired volleys of bullets into the air, celebrating or protesting (I forget which) some cause I will never understand. Edward was uninterested. All I could think of was what would happen to the bullets, when they fell to earth, long after the memory of their firing was gone. Would someone, miles away, who knew just as little about that particular struggle, get hurt?

Tomorrow, Mr Sudbury will stay for nine minutes. As he hops aboard the London-bound train, the door clunking solidly behind him, my life will never be the same again.

Reet lasted pretty much two years to the day. Two years after Father's suicide, Edward was on the doorstep. We never discussed it; he just came back in and carried on his life of shifting coal. There were no children; for that the barber can be thanked. Edward never explained what had gone sour, but I guessed. Rita made it back into the papers the following year, scandalising the town again with her marriage to a recently excommunicated Catholic priest. The artful cut of her dress, I was told, nearly concealed the swelling of her belly.

I have just one photograph of my mother. Cameras were for rich people then. I look at it now, in its tarnished frame, on the mantelpiece in the sitting-room. I am dressed for work, wearing the lightweight synthetic uniform which these days expresses our corporate image.

The expression captured in my mother's eyes (how old must I have been then? Five, six? Less than ten) is one of weariness. She looks to me as though she understands. I am sure my mother understands.

In a little over an hour's time, Mr Sudbury will arrive.

My walk to work takes me (as it has always taken me) past the derelict Station Hotel. This morning, for the first time in years, I think of Father. I am tired. The sleeplessness of my night reminds me of him too. The solicitor who dealt with the will and probate said (with due embarrassment) that Father had timed it to perfection. The redundancy money paid off the rest of the mortgage. There would, of course, be no insurance money; not with that 'mode of death'. But Edward and I would inherit the house.

I was ten when my mother disappeared from my life. For months I wrote her letters in my drawing pad, and drew her pictures also, begging her to come home. I didn't know how to get them to her. Father found them. Wine, beer; Bill lad, come here. Come and give your old man a kiss. She's never coming back, Bill. She's never coming back.

The Nottingham-bound train squeals to a halt. Mr Sudbury's patent shoes scrunch on the platform as he alights. In his hand he holds a brightly wrapped box. He is the only passenger, and not a customer either.

'So, Butler, a sad day for us all,' he sings out as he nears me. He keeps on walking, and I fall in beside, the two of us heading for the footbridge which will take us to the other side, and he to his London-bound train.

'You do understand,' he says as we take the first steps two at a time. 'Open stations are the future. It's the way it has to be.'

He pauses, smiles, then carries on climbing. 'Anyway, a great opportunity for you to develop some new interests.'

We descend to the other platform and stand by the white border at its edge. I repainted it earlier in the year. Mr Sudbury talks of cricket, of the coming tour to the Caribbean. Eight minutes pass. As the London-bound train draws up, he gives me the package.

'Nothing much, but a heartfelt token of appreciation for all the years of service you've given the railway.'

I take it from him and stand, waiting for him to embark. He doesn't move. The silence smoulders, but I can't think of anything to say.

'Well, man, go on. Aren't you going to open it?'

I place the box on the platform and crouch down, wrestling briefly with the sellotape. Inside is a carriage clock, gilded and with hands and numbers that look as though they will glow in the dark, making it easy to mark the passing hours.

Father's suicide note told the police exactly where to look. The digging lasted just two days. Two days to find my mother, who I had never found with all my letters and all my drawings. I read in the paper that Father had cut her up in the shed, with his kitchen knife and a saw. He crammed her into a chest in which we'd kept our toys when young. Wine, beer; Bill lad, come here. Come and give your old man a kiss.

I know the neighbours gossiped, found it strange that I should stay in 'that house'. But I never abandoned her, nor she me. She stares out at the sitting-room, understanding that all life's happiness is merely tragedy in the making.

'You'll be all right, financially?'

Mr Sudbury is talking again. His expression makes me want to laugh. It looks as though he may have practised it in front of the mirror.

'Yes,' I tell him, 'I'll manage.'

'Good, good. Well,' he turns towards the train and grasps the nearest door handle, 'must be off. Cheerio, Butler. All the best.'

He's halfway into the carriage before I say: 'Mr Sudbury?'

He twists round. 'Mmm?'

'I do have them. Interests, I mean.'

'Oh, good. That's good, Butler.'

'I'm interested in lots of things. Crows and ants and aphids . . .'

'Gardening? Jolly good, well . . .'

'And chefs and knives and how . . .'

The guard's whistle is shrill.

'Look, Butler, I really must . . .'

'And another thing, Mr Sudbury . . .'

He stares at me.

'What do you think, I mean: when a bullet is fired in the air, what do you think happens to it?'

'I . . . Are you all right, Butler?'

Slowly I nod and squeeze the carriage clock, the sides digging into my palms. He waits just a moment then slams the door. The train pulls out, bound for London.

I watch it depart, yellow end eventually passing out of sight. Later on, when my last day's work is done, I walk back, past the derelict Station Hotel, to Edward, our house, his love of television soaps and his life shovelling coal.

Joe O'Donnell
Joe O'Donnell is a free-lance writer and TV director. His short stories have been published and broadcast and he has written for TV, radio and theatre. His radio play, *Silver Side of the Mirror*, won the EBU Premio Ondas award and he is currently one of the writers of the children's TV series *The Morbegs*.

Aleksandra Lech
Aleks Lech was born in Surrey, where she grew up. She studied theatre design at Wimbledon School of Art, and later attended the National Film & Television School in Beaconsfield. She lives and works in London.

Patrick Cunningham
Patrick Cunningham was born in Wexford, Ireland and now lives in south-west London. His stories have been published in *The European, New Irish Writing, Woman's Journal, Panurge, Jennings Magazine, Iron* and in the anthology *Smoke Signals*. Three of his stories have been read on BBC Radio 4. He was a prize-winner in The London Arts short story competition, the London Writers competition, the Swanage Arts Festival and the West Sussex competition, and received a Hennessy Award for short story writing.

Ros Barber
Ros Barber was born in 1964 in Washington D.C., and brought up in Essex. Having trained as a biologist and worked as a cleaner, a barmaid, an office temp and an analyst programmer, she now teaches creative writing part-time at the University of Sussex. A prize-winning poet, she was awarded a major bursary by South East Arts for her first novel, which is nearing completion. Her first collection of short stories is likely to be published next year.

Charles Lambert
Charles Lambert was born and brought up in the Midlands. After reading English literature at Cambridge, he travelled around Ireland, Portugal and Italy. Since 1982, he has been living in Rome, where he works as a university teacher, translator and freelance journalist. He has published stories in anthologies published by Third House and in Paris Transcontinental, as well as poetry in small magazines in Britain and the US.

Judi Moore
Judi was born and brought up in Cornwall, where she worked as a typist with the local council for six years before absconding to university. Thereafter she worked as a crisis manager for the Open University. She now writes full time. She lives in a Tardis-like, Edwardian terraced house in the new town of Milton Keynes with five cats and a dog.

R.D. Malagola
Rob Malagola, born in Rome and brought up in west London, now lives in a small Wiltshire town with his partner and their two children. He has lived and worked in many parts of the world and been involved in a variety of occupations, including

Contributors' Notes

theatre work, design and the NHS. His short story, *South*, was written in a tent in south-western France during the summer of 1996.

Adèle Geras

Adèle Geras was born in Jerusalem in 1944. She has published more than fifty books for children and young adults, including *A Lane to the Land of the Dead* (Puffin): a collection of ghost stories set in Manchester, where she has lived for the past thirty years. Her latest book is *The Orchard Book of Short Stories* (Orchard) illustrated by nine different artists.

Amy Prior

Amy Prior was born in 1970 and lives in London. She is a graduate of Manchester University and has a post-graduate teaching qualification from London University. She has worked as a copy editor and a teacher of adults and children, and has travelled extensively throughout the United States. Her fiction has been published in *Fission* and *Allnighter* (Pulp Faction), and she is currently working on a collection of short stories.

David Croft

David Croft was born in Batley, West Yorkshire in 1964 and is a graduate of Jacob Kramer College of Art. He has lived in Dublin for the past five years where he works as an Art Director in the advertising industry. Previously published work includes poetry in *Cyphers, Envoi, Lifelines, W.P. Monthly* and *The Haiku Quarterly*. He is currently working on his first collection of short stories.

Angus Calder

Angus Calder taught at the University of Nairobi from 1968 to 1971 during which time his historical study *The People's War: Britain 1939–1945* was published. He has since published widely on historical and literary topics. His first volume of verse, *Waking in Waikato*, has just appeared from Diehard (1997) and this is his first published short story.

Penny Simpson

After graduating from Brighton Art College and Essex University, Penny Simpson moved to Cardiff where she has worked as a journalist, theatre reviewer and lecturer. In 1993, she received a bursary from the Arts Council of Wales to write her first novel. She's currently working on a second book, whilst studying British Sign Language and lecturing at the Glamorgan Centre of Art & Design Technology.

Amanda Coe

Amanda Coe grew up in South Yorkshire and Canada. She read English at Oxford University and screenwriting at the National Film and Television School. She writes regularly for television.

Phil Whitaker

Phil Whitaker was born in Kent in 1966. He studied medicine at Nottingham and now works as a part time general practitioner in Oxford where he lives with his wife Lynn. Phil's debut novel, *Eclipse of the Sun*, was published by Phoenix House in August 1997.